"Damn, boy, you can WRITE.

"I can't tell you how much fun I had reading this piece ["Black Wind"]. It is spot on and solid as solid can be. Loved the setup, and the sure hand you used telling the tale. Loved the character of Hull, and that crackling perfectly understated dialogue you put in his mouth. Great landscape, great descriptions . . . loved the spent shells sparking like fool's gold, the sheriff papering his makings like a spider wrapping a paralyzed grub, the wind beating the last ghost of white paint off the clapboard schoolhouse, a bunch of other stuff that made me contemplate literary thievery. And when you unleashed that horde at the end. . . .

"Yep. Great job cinching the saddle on that sucker and bucking it across the page. Solid stuff, and you have my congrats."

—Norman Partridge, Bram Stoker Award-winning author of
Dark Harvest and *The Man with the Barbed-Wire Fists*

"It doesn't matter if he's doing crime, Lovecraftian short stories, strange literary fiction disguised as madman narratives, horror or something in between, you always get an explosive mixture of ideas and superb use of language when reading Cody Goodfellow."

—Gabino Iglesias, Shirley Jackson Award-winning author
of *Coyote Songs* and *The Devil Takes You Home*

"Cody Goodfellow's imagination is a freeway flyer, and his prose is a ride on a rocket sled. He's one of the two or three best god-damned writers in the genres today."

—Michael Shea, World Fantasy Award-winning author of
Nifft the Lean and "The Autopsy"

"Cody Goodfellow knows how to chill your blood."

—Stephen King

The Greedy Grave

The Greedy Grave

❖

Tales of Inigo Hull

Cody Goodfellow

Hippocampus Press

New York

Published by Hippocampus Press
P.O. Box 641, New York, NY 10156.
www.hippocampuspress.com

Hippocampus Press logo designed by Anastasia Damianakos.

First Edition
1 3 5 7 9 8 6 4 2

ISBN 978-1-61498-484-9 paperback
ISBN 978-1-61498-489-4 ebook

Contents

The Greedy Grave

The sun brought only a deeper chill when it rose above the lavender peaks enclosing the Great Basin, drawing traces of damp from sour soil, stirring a bitter winter wind and shedding its pale pink light on sights better left unseen.

Inigo Hull returned to camp at dawn to find Ed Schaffroth, Elmer Braden, and Buck Marriot already awake and in a high state of excitement with the discovery that the fifth member of their expedition had his throat cut and scalp taken sometime in the night.

"I told you and I told you!" Braden was shouting. "The damned curse ain't even waiting for us to dig it up."

"Ain't no curse," Marriot snapped, spitting a brown gob of tobacco juice into the ashes. "This here's still Shoshone country . . ."

Schaffroth saw the half-Comanche tracker riding up and lifted his rifle to coax him off his mount. "Here comes a simpler explanation," he said, his dour mouth pinched so severely that it could be seen out from under the drooping wings of his mustache.

Hull climbed down from his red and white palomino and approached the body of Bob Resley where it slouched over the dying embers of the campfire. Resley, a backslider Mormon prospector out of Utah, had taken the last watch of the night and had plainly been murdered near the end of it while making coffee. Person or persons unknown had cut his throat and taken his scalp, indeed his whole face, leaving only the red *me-*

mento mori of bare, crimson bone to greet his comrades.

"If the Shoshone set upon you," Hull said, "they wouldn't creep in and take one man. They would take every horse and mule and all your guns without disturbing your sleep. None of you would've woken up at all.

"As for myself . . . I can't figure why I'd want to whittle down your numbers when I could've just taken off after the gold myself. Why don't you paint the picture for me?"

"Maybe you don't hear so good," Schaffroth said, cocking an eyebrow at the scarry concavity where someone once chopped off one of the tracker's ears. "It's all there in plain red." Schaffroth pointed at Resley's naked skull. "You went out to scout up the spot, you found it, and figured you'd take a bigger share for yourself, maybe scare the rest of us off and take the whole lode for yourself."

Hull was a man ill inclined toward moments of levity, but the grave accusation almost brought a smile to his grim, scarred face. "And maybe I did away with your other friend, Watt, when you weren't watching me cut a trail out from Fort Ruby. Maybe there's two of me."

The men had been on edge from the start, like any party of strangers bound only by the lust for gold. They set out from Fort Ruby only three days ago. The mountains had proved slow going, as trails went dead in tortuous box canyons, off sheer bluffs, or into brush as thick as the hair on an Indian's head. Hull knew the land well enough and had scouted the landmarks that led to what these men sought, but he also knew the Shoshone legends about this stretch of the Ruby Mountains, where the terrain was said to change like a blanket thrown over a restless sleeper.

"Maybe there *are* two of you," Schaffroth said impatiently. "You're here for a share of the gold, same as any of us. Maybe you already have it. Maybe you just kept us alive to dig it up for you."

"And maybe *I'm* only alive because I haven't led you to it yet," Hull said. He leaned over Resley and took the fine brass telescope the dead prospector kept in the breast pocket of his potato-sack coat. He looked through it, tapped it, and looked again, puzzled that it conveyed no wondrous powers of magnification at all.

Marriot took the coffee off its cradle of charred sticks, shook it to hear the slosh of a half-full pot, and grumbled, "Hope the poor bastard left us a decent pot of coffee for once."

Hull knew he could trust none of them any more than they trusted him. Ed Schaffroth was a foreman at the Bar S Ranch. Braden and Marriot were two of his hired hands. Schaffroth was the one who heard the legend from Resley, who'd panned for gold from California to Texas and come up with only tall tales. It was enough to set their minds on fire with dreams of hidden gold in these godforsaken mountains.

Schaffroth and Resley approached Hull with Lionel Watt, a quiet, dapper type with a pianist's hands and gunslinger's dead gray eyes, who acted like another hired hand, but Hull reckoned he represented the money that backed this misadventure. Watt let Schaffroth bark all he liked while gently holding the leash. The Bar S was more of a plantation than a ranch, the owner famous for tying up his hands in debt-bondage and beating them like slaves when they came up short.

Hull's suspicion became certainty when Watt was the first to die.

In his years with the Comanche, the Union Cavalry, and as a bounty hunter and tracker, Inigo Hull had seen more than his share of scalped men, women, and children, but the violence visited upon Watt's remains went beyond the cruel but practical collection of a trophy or proof of a bounty. Whoever killed

Watt and Resley took each man's scalp and skin down to the chin while he sat watch over the sleeping camp. Hull, who had ridden ahead to search the hills for landmarks by moonlight for reasons he refused to explain, was charged with the foul deeds, but their entirely justified fear of Hull had prevailed where their faith in reason had not. That, and their lust for gold.

No Indians under the sun, or even the most depraved white men, took such trophies. But the gold they were after came with a curse that hearkened to a race of Indians who were long gone when the sun itself was young.

According to the legend, the Spaniards who came to Ruby Valley in the late sixteenth century were desperate, seizing upon every tribe they encountered for rumors of Cibola, of El Dorado, of another Machu Picchu or Tenochtitlan. Canny Indians fed them enough lies to send them over the next mountain range, where the legend was added to and spiked with whatever fabulous details they could concoct to keep the gold-mad conquistadors searching somewhere else.

So it was inevitable that when they finally met a Shoshone chief who foolishly showed them a medallion of pure, flawless gold the size of his palm, they took him captive and tortured him for the secret of its source.

He told them that an ancestor many generations past had taken it in trade from the men of the Shadow Cities. They placed little value on gold, for they knew the secret of making it; but no one had seen them since the world was young. But more than that, on his life, he could not tell, for their splendid cities lay far beneath the surface of the earth, and all their secret roads had long since been swallowed up.

Mad with greed and bedeviled by years of fruitless questing after phantoms, the Spaniards buried the chief up to his neck and starved him, and when he was delirious with hunger they began to feed him raw meat and deluge him with icy mountain water, which made him sick.

After weeks of torment the chief surrendered and agreed to draw a map to the cavern where the unclaimed gold of the Shadow Cities lay buried, not a day's journey from their encampment. With a sharp rock he inscribed the location on the gold medallion itself and asked to be reunited with his family.

At this, his cruel captors laughed and explained to him what he had been eating during his captivity. The chief submitted to add a crucial detail to the map, but then he spoke a curse upon the gold and any who sought it, and swallowed it.

Vexed beyond reason, the Spaniards beat the chief to death and cut open his belly, but were somehow unable to find the gold coin. They threw his broken body into a shallow grave and resolved to quit their doomed quest; but their leader, an ambitious disinherited noble facing ruin at home, returned to the grave to dig up the Shoshone chief and recover the gold coin.

Not even his compatriots knew what became of the desecrator, but their tale ended with the unedifying observation that the grave simply ate him, and his demoralized henchmen faded away into history's shameful backwaters.

It was the longest of long shots, a hope resting on a shadowy legend that promised only doom and misfortune, but there was already little else left to chase in this prematurely domesticated state more enclosed by rancher's fences every day, whose booming silver mines offered only the chance to make another man rich.

Hull turned from these confusing eddies of morbid fancy to the question of the telescope. The prospector had precious little to show for his years of treasure-hunting, but why would anyone just take the glass out of it?

"You'd better find it before sundown today," Schaffroth

said, "or we won't wait to see who gets scalped next."

Hull studied the landmark against which they'd made camp—an outcropping of yellow-white boulders that jutted out of the mouth of a narrow ravine. Utterly unlike the surrounding stones, the postpile culminated in a wall of fluted spires like chimneys or minarets, almost a hundred feet above the gentle slope where they camped.

He'd had to ride in ever-widening circles for most of the night before he found the next landmark about half a mile away, beside which he'd bedded down without incident for the few hours of rest he needed. He had sketched in these peculiar landscape features on a recent but worse-than-useless survey map, and he had a fair notion of where their final destination lay, despite the terrain's best efforts to defy him. It would be best if he got them there before dark for all kinds of reasons, before any more of them went missing.

"I know this land better than any of you," Hull said, "and better than most Shoshone. If I wanted the gold for myself, I'd never have brought you along. I don't expect you to believe me, but if you want to make something of it, you're welcome to try."

"I don't see why we shouldn't," Schaffroth said. "He's probably got them redskins all lined up to bushwhack us, soon as we've dug up the gold."

"All I'll tell you," Hull said, "is that I'm not a greedy man."

"Damn, this coffee's bitter," Marriot said, but he bolted it down and went to pour another cup. Just then Hull dropped the telescope and barked, "Don't drink it!" He went to knock the pot out of his hands, but the ranchhand dropped it all on his own.

Marriot reached out for Hull, to choke him or to plead for help. The next words from his lips were drowned in a gusher of blood.

Schaffroth and Braden recoiled in horror, but Hull took hold of Marriot and smelled his dying breath. It had no odor, but Hull deduced, correctly if too late, that the crystal lenses in the prospector's telescope had been ground up and added to the morning coffee.

"I told you!" Braden shouted, "told you and told you . . ."

"Braden's right," Hull said. "Sure as shit there's a curse on us, but Indians got nothing to do with it."

The depleted expedition led its string of riderless horses and pack mules up the ravine beyond the odd outcropping, Braden regaling them all the way with Indian ghost stories. With his own two eyes he'd seen a redskin woman glowing like the moon, standing by night on the top of one of those mysterious mounds in Kansas, waving and beckoning though she had no head; and the tales he told of the Shadow Cities were more far-fetched still, but the Indians who told them to him feared those bygone people as much as white men loved gold.

The undulating land took its toll on them, eating up the day. They followed the steep, treacherous ravine up to a false peak that gave out in a snarl of canyons. Hull chose their path after some hesitation, wishing he had Resley's telescope.

"Maybe he don't know the way after all," Braden sneered.

"I'm waiting on our other man," Hull said.

"Now hold on," Schaffroth said. "Don't try to complicate things. Right now only one man had the motive and the means to do what you did to Resley and Watt."

"And put on a pot of ground-glass coffee to do for the rest of you," Braden put in.

"Maybe so," Schaffroth said.

"Maybe a simpler explanation," Hull said. "Maybe this party trailed us from Fort Ruby and came into camp night before last, and Mr. Watt didn't raise the alarm because he was expected."

Schaffroth vividly disapproved of where this was going, but he didn't interrupt again.

"Maybe this other one answered to you, and maybe he answered to the same fellow who pays Watt's wages, which I reckon would be the owner of the Bar S. You didn't seem all that busted up when Watt turned up dead."

"I won't go broke buying flowers if either of you cayuses turn up dead tomorrow," Schaffroth said, "but it don't add up to nothing."

"Not by itself, I freely allow," Hull answered. "You didn't even concern yourself with burying him under those rocks and brush, but Elmer here did."

"Don't drag me into this," Braden said.

"You notice his hands?" Hull asked.

"I noticed his head, and how it had no damned face."

"His fingers were short and hairy," Hull said. "Watt had long, fine fingers, and he kept his nails short and clean. Man we buried was wearing Watt's fine broadcloth suit, but he had hands like an ape."

Schaffroth scowled, but his eyes were wide and suddenly searching the broken land around them with barely suppressed panic.

"So you see, it's pretty simple. There was an outside man in our camp that night, and he and Mr. Watt were reading from the same book. But not from the same page."

The trail forked again. Hull stopped, looking up at the sun. "Next landmark is just ahead."

"What about the coffee?" Braden demanded.

Hull shook his head. He didn't come out this far from people to have to talk so damn much. "Maybe Resley figured he didn't much care who was killing who over what, and thought he'd put you all down and split the take with me when I came back as the sole survivor.

"All I know is, I'd think twice before I let a Mormon make my coffee."

It was nearly noon when they came into sight of the next landmark, a badly weathered hoodoo rearing up out of a jumble of shattered granite on the opposite face of the canyon. It was of the same pitted, yellow-white stone and similar even in formation, with a row of crooked columns scraping at the ruthlessly blue sky, like the pipes of an organ atop a base of tightly packed boulders.

Braden uneasily stared at it as they rode closer and seemed to shy away from crossing its shadow, but Schaffroth watched the rising ridgetops with his rifle braced across the horn of his saddle. "Is this it?" he demanded.

"No, but it's close by." He pointed at a depression in the soft sand above the hoodoo, where a small campfire had been kicked in and thoroughly buried. "Where I camped last night," he said.

"That's no alibi," Schaffroth shot back.

Hull rode up a winding draw that broke out of the enclosing ridges, so the setting sun fell full upon his profile. Schaffroth watched him, hesitating, then rode up alongside him.

"What makes you believe this story is even true, let alone worth killing for?" Hull asked.

Schaffroth was just surprised enough by the question to answer it. "It just feels true. You look out on these mountains and you can just feel that vitality, that power, that wealth, locked up in it, waiting for you to rip it out and strike it rich. Those dumb redskins been sitting on it all this time, doing not a damned thing with it. Be better off when they're all gone."

"Conquistadors couldn't find gold in this country . . . they couldn't even find gold in one dead Indian."

Schaffroth snapped his fingers. "And there's the rub, damn it. That old Shoshone chief pulled a fast one on those idiots, like a riverboat magician. All I know is, them Spaniards went away empty-handed, and the Shoshone sure as hell don't have it, but whether it's somewhere in his guts or tucked away in the highest goddamn tree on this here mountain, I aim to find it."

The mountaintop was a cracked dome of the same uncanny white rock, eroded and hollowed out so the trail ended in a roofless grotto with only a few stunted pines and knots of scrub. The dirt underfoot was hard as baked adobe in all but one patch dead center in the eerie canyon. The rock walls curled over them in jagged, serried formations that reminded even the stolid Schaffroth of gigantic teeth. The ranch foreman stood behind Hull when he dished out the shovels. The tracker didn't need to be told he had a rifle aimed at his back.

"Unless there really are two of you," Schaffroth said, "you best take up a shovel and commence to digging."

Hull shook his head, but joined Elmer Braden in turning over the soft dirt that was the only sensible place hereabouts, to dig a grave.

"Damn conniving half-breed," Schaffroth grated. "Think you're two steps ahead of everybody."

Hull put his back into shoveling, into a rhythm that complemented the slower, less deliberate labor of the older, heavier ranchhand at his side.

"No more smart talk, Mr. Consulting Detective? Got our brains all stirred with that talk about some other fella on our trail, working the outside, when it's been you all along."

"I was just wondering when Mr. Watt would come to collect for his boss. There's still a lot of work to do yet, even if that gold coin does turn up in the grave, even if there is a map, even if any of that legend is true . . ."

"And what would you know about it?"

"I'd know it was a lie, if I was the one who spread it around . . ."

Schaffroth jumped to his feet and raised his rifle. "What the hell're you talking about? You better hope this ain't some wild goose chase—"

The next thing to come out of Schaffroth's mouth was the back of his skull. The poleaxed foreman stumbled a moment, transfixed by the echoing thunderclap of the shot that killed him.

"Oh, you snake-blooded, two-faced, half-breed sonofabitch," Braden said.

"Bite your tongue," Hull said. "You got no idea how many faces I wear." He looked up to spot the wisp of smoke from among the jagged overhanging rocks. "Just keep digging."

By and by a slim, soiled, but still dapper figure, even in homespun secondhand clothes, came down out of the rocks with a rifle and a pistol trained on them.

"Evening, Mr. Watt," Hull said. "Care to take up a shovel?"

"I'm better suited to this kind of iron," Watt said, casually weighing the Winchester in one hand and the bone-handled Colt revolver in the other. "You all seem to have the job well in hand. I wouldn't dream of interrupting with my inexpert contributions."

Hull nodded and resumed digging. They were knee-deep in a wide hole, and the shovelfuls of earth came easier and faster all the time. Braden was ruddy and gleaming with sweat. He finally threw down his shovel. "You may as well know," he shouted, "this-here snake made up the whole thing!"

"What's this, now?" Watt asked. He'd set the rifle down and

was rolling a cigarette one-handed while dangling the revolver by its trigger-guard. "Why would you get these boys' hopes up with a tall tale? If we don't find no Indian in yonder grave, we just gonna have to leave one . . ."

Hull kept digging. "There's a Shoshone chief buried right here. That much is true. His name was Woshiute of the Mahaguaduka Seed Eater band of the Western Shoshone nation. But he wasn't killed three hundred years ago by Spaniards over gold. He was killed twenty years ago by Union cavalry officers trying to take the only gold he possessed."

"The coin?" Braden wheezed. "Well, it was still a fair hunk of gold . . ."

"The land," Hull said, "was all the gold he had, and they wanted it all."

Watt cocked his pistol and lit his cigarette. "Both of you, keep digging. And you . . . half-breed. Keep talking."

Hull obeyed, talking as he dug. "They took Woshiute prisoner, beat him, broke his limbs and buried him up to his neck, starved him to make him sign a treaty surrendering the whole Ruby Valley. Woshiute could no more give away the land than he could give away the stars, but he was willing to give it his body. When he wouldn't do it even as he neared death by hunger, they began to feed him meat. At first it made him sick, but then he began to crave it, to cry out for it in a voice that they found amusing at first, but then came to hate and fear.

"For the cavalry officers had raided Woshiute's village and slaughtered his whole band—babies with brains dashed out on rocks, women raped and gutted like fish, children scalped and impaled on blazing stakes . . . and they had been feeding them to Woshiute.

"They had all but forgotten what they came for, so lost were they in their own evil, in the evil they'd created. Woshiute only laughed when they told him what he'd been eating, because he'd known all along, and by this time the Shoshone chief was no longer the man he was. For one thing, he'd been growing. He kept threatening to break out, so they piled the dirt on top of him until only his face looked up from the bottom of a wide grave, but every time they filled it, somehow, he emptied it."

"I don't want to hear it," Braden said.

"I do," Watt said. "I'll get paid the same, whatever you boys find or don't. For that matter, so will you. So how much did this ol' Shoshone chief eat, anyway?"

"In the end, they fed every last corpse, forty-seven men, women, and children, into the hole, but the chief wasn't satisfied. He'd sign the treaty, he said, if they only set him free. A few of them filled in the hole and went away to try to forget what they'd seen, what they'd fed and created."

"And what was that, boy?" Watt asked.

Hull stopped digging and fixed the hired killer with his flinty eyes. "A Wendigo," he said.

Braden stopped digging, shifting his feet uneasily in the hole, which had begun to fill in with mud. "Judas get home, that's strange . . ." he observed, but no one took notice.

Hull pointed at his saddlebag on the flank of his red-white palomino. Watt went over and dug out the map. Hull stepped out of the hole as he came over, tapping on the marked-up survey. "So that pile of rocks back there—"

"Where you killed Resley?"

"Yes, indeed. What was it?"

"One of his feet."

Watt twisted his lips into a smile. "Do tell. And that other one over yonder, about half a mile away as the crow flies . . ."

"His left hand. They decayed pretty fast once they were exposed."

Chuckling in disbelief, the gunslinger traced the outline sketched over a map, the stick figure delineated by the exposed hand and foot, leading to the craggy, rudimentary mouth drawn over the mountaintop. "He sure did grow awful big in, what, twenty years? Eating all those Indians . . ."

"He's been fed a lot more than forty-seven people," Hull admitted. "In the years since he's been down there, not even I know how many treasure hunters have come to dig up his grave, but he welcomes them. He's become what the Algonquian call *wendigo*, and he knows only hunger."

This was finally too much for Watt's indulgent character. "You sayin' he's still *alive* down there?"

"I am saying only that he is still hungry."

So engrossed had Watt been in the map's fanciful embellishments that he didn't notice until now that Braden was gone, leaving his shovel standing upright in the mud.

Watt took up the shovel, noticing how the hole tapered but never terminated, the blackness at its bottom gobbling up the clods and pebbles knocked loose by his boots. "Where the hell did that no-account get off to?"

Hull looked up at the moon rising up above the jagged walls of the canyon. "You know what happened to him."

"Horseshit," Watt said, probing the edge of the hole with the shovel, gun poised, mesmerized by the illusion of a great, gray wave down in the blackness, softly lapping at the earth from a vast space beneath his feet. "You're a bigger damn liar than that chiseling foreman, that poisoning prospector, or the other chowderhead who got himself lost right under my nose."

"I have not lied to you," Hull said. "And I only lied to them once."

The walls of the canyon shuddered, shedding rocks. The walls of the grave shivered, the hole widening on its own. Watt took a clumsy step backwards, still staring down into it as if it contained treasure, after all. "When was that? When you told them about the gold?"

"I didn't have to do that," Hull said. "I lied when I told them I wasn't a greedy man." He struck Watt over the head with the shovel and pushed the gunslinger into the gurgling throat.

"I sorely wish," Hull said, "that I had more of you to feed him."

Broken Bell

1

The sun at high noon was a curse on the earth when the exhausted pinto mare that bore Lope Obregon and Eight-Finger Nate into the dooryard of the long-forgotten mission dropped dead under their weight. The two men slashed their saddlebags free of the dead horse and ran for the arched doorway at the foot of the bone-white church, and the gaunt, hooded figure that stood in its shadow as if awaiting the desperate men.

"Bless me, padre, for I have sinned," said Lope Obregon, crossing himself while his partner drew his mismatched pistols. "We claim sanctuary . . ."

Hoofbeats clattered up the narrow ridge that spilled out into the bad, broken valley in which the mission was the only sign of humankind for two days' ride in any direction, and a welcome surprise. One might almost say a miracle.

Nate aimed to shoot down the rider, but Obregon barked, "Put down your guns, you fool. They have no choice but to take us in."

The rider came over the ridge bent low behind a painted stallion, guns drawn, reins in his teeth. Nate shook off his partner and let fly, taking the horse in its breast and rippling neck. The stallion stumbled and spilled its rider just on the far side of a crooked wall of adobe bricks framing the dooryard of the mission.

The rider rolled out of the saddle as the horse fell, taking shelter behind the wall and putting one bullet in the horse's brain with his right while nicking Nate's ear with the luckiest of three shots from his left. "Come afoot or in a bag from the neck up, it's all the same to me!" came the shout from the far side of the well.

"Sanctuary!" cried Obregon, and a few words in an Indian tongue that bandits on the border used as oaths.

The hooded monk bowed his head and opened the double doors of the mission. "All are welcome to San Demetrio," he said.

"They're wanted in three territories for rape, murder, rustling, and worse," the rider shouted.

"He's just a half-breed bounty-hunter," said Nate, pressing a bandana to the gory hole in his ear, "and a damn liar in the bargain. All we are to him is a fat reward."

"You will take a vow and live in the service of our Lord," said the monk.

"You've got to the count of ten to come out," shouted the bounty hunter, "and I'm just past seven!"

"Go to hell, Hull!" Nate shouted. "We done got born again!"

Obregon knelt before the monk and kissed the hem of his robe of woven human hair. "I take communion, I confess my many sins. I will . . . we will serve the Lord and his son Jesus Christ——"

The monk took hold of Obregon's hair and jerked his head back to bare his throat and hold the blade of an obsidian knife to it. Before the bandit or his partner could respond, the tolling of a solitary bell echoed from the tapered tower. A doleful sound that reverberated through every cavity of the body and the marrow of every bone, it stopped time and erased thought, ironed flat any illusion of free will.

"You will learn the name of *our* Lord," said the monk, "and serve Him for all eternity." Smiling to reveal only a toothless hole, he put away his knife. Lifting the bandit to his feet like an empty gourd, the monk ushered the bandits through the open door. Both humbly shuffled along in a trance, and not far behind them came the bounty hunter, his trembling guns forgotten in his hands.

As he crossed the threshold, Inigo Hull the bounty hunter might have taken notice of the fresh hole in the whitewashed adobe façade of the mission where one of his stray bullets had hit home only moments before.

But if he saw the strange bricks exposed by the fissure in the wall, the jumble of cloven skulls and splintered limbs embedded in the crumbling mortar, he gave no sign. He only bowed his head as he passed through the door behind the men he'd been hunting, meekly removing his hat and sleepwalking into darkness as the heavy oaken door closed and was barred behind him.

Most of the men Inigo Hull hunted he would just as soon have let ramble, if not for the bounty. Most laws they broke were the quaint daydreams of the east, with no purchase on the realities out west. But Eight-Finger Nate's gang was a breed apart and operated like it, burning down men, women, and children like livestock.

Hull had been pursuing Obregon and Tate for the better part of a week as they careened westward from a stagecoach robbery outside Flagstaff. He'd dogged them across Nevada into the Humboldts, where Nate McKeever tried to go to ground among his people, only he was caught by territorial marshals in Warpaint. His gang burned down the schoolhouse to decoy his escape, killing four children and the schoolmarm, and tried to cross the desert into California with an angry posse on their tail. After a hot time in Yuma, only Obregon and McKeever

were still alive, but they outfoxed the posse, who pursued a
dead trail over the border and doubled back west, into the broken Mojave and the Valley of Death.

Hull had picked up their tracks in the mountains and kept
on them until Nate's horse dropped dead and they had to ride
pillion. He'd driven his own horse past saving to catch them
and expected it to end in one crooked arroyo or another south
of the Sierra Nevada, but they had come instead upon this mission where no such thing should be, and certainly not one still
in the hands of the Church.

Hull had hours in which to pace his cell and search for a
way out, while his mind pondered too late the question of how
he came to be here. He had intended to call out the monk who
offered the two bandits sanctuary, but instead had meekly followed them in, surrendering his guns to the leather-faced man
in a hooded cassock who stood inside the doorway.

Fray Joachim said nothing as he led Hull to the featureless
room of whitewashed adobe. The window was too high to
reach and too small to squeeze through, even if he could break
the rusted iron bars.

"You cannot escape," said a voice from the shadowy corner
of the room beneath and beside the window. Speaking in archaic, oddly accented Spanish, the voice added, "You do not
even know how you came to be here, do you?"

Hull squinted and took a step back. He'd seen and heard no
one until his cellmate spoke. Even now, he seemed to be blinded
by the sunlight through the bars, for the shape of the speaker
never came any clearer.

"They may drive Indians like stock, but they're not hard
men," Hull muttered, staring out the side of his eyes at the
shadow. "Those eggs I'm after will hop the fence and lam out
first chance they get, and me after them."

"No one has," said the voice, "in over three hundred years. No one."

Hull resisted arguing, for there was no point. He could argue with himself about why he'd let himself be locked up, but his wits seemed to go to water when he was confronted with the monk.

He recalled the tolling of the bell like rings of iron laid on his neck, bowing his head so he could not look the monk in the eye as the latter introduced himself. "I am Fray Joachim, and I welcome you into the service of our lord. You will toil and reap his plenty and thereby earn salvation from the curses of all mortal flesh. As you work and pray, so you will be fed and sheltered."

He did not even need to order Hull to turn over his weapons. Somehow the command came in the sound of the bell or the weight of his gaze. Even now, Hull's hands itched for iron, yet he somehow knew they would fail him when the time came round again.

Only when he finally knuckled under and lay down to watch the light fail did a shuffling pair of sandals stop outside his cell. He crouched in the corner of the cell behind the door. "When do they feed us?"

"Eat nothing they give you," said the voice, as a key turned in the lock. "Do not take the darkness into your mouth . . ."

Fray Joachim stood in the doorway. Hull was halfway to his feet when the bell tolled. Every nerve throbbed in agony, and he seemed to watch down the wrong end of a telescope as his body sleepwalked past the friar, who held a lamp to light his way in the gloom.

It took everything he had to look over his shoulder and see if his cellmate was following them. Hull felt himself flinch away from the monk as if his displeasure was the edge of a cliff, but the monk chuckled and obligingly held the lamp higher to shine into every corner of his cell. In the corner where his cellmate sat, Hull saw only a mound of yellow dust and a few fragments of what might once have been bones.

The bell tolled again and Hull followed the monk out into the cloister, where McKeever and Obregon shuffled in nervous circles beside a barefoot peasant in tatters. All avoided his eyes, but he saw in them what he most dreaded to find in his own. No law, not even the law of the gun, would keep them peaceful. Nate McKeever once took a warden's wife and children hostage to escape a prison in Flagstaff, but even he seemed to itch all over with the command to be meek as a mayor in church on election day.

They followed Fray Joachim across the cloister and down a crooked corridor to a wide, low-ceilinged dining hall. Hull took a seat across from the others on a bench with deep grooves worn into the wood. A basket of blood-red corn kernels, carelessly roasted, sat in the center of the table, and four clay cups of water. There were no utensils, only dented tin plates that someone nailed to the table.

Across a host of empty tables—enough to seat maybe sixty or more—sat half a dozen cowled monks at a long, elevated banquet table, their hands lost in their sleeves. In the dim light that came from the lamp Fray Joachim set on the end of their table as he took his chair, they seemed only to move by a trick of the light.

"I ain't eating this shit," growled Eight-Finger Nate. Reaching for his cup, he cast a sour look at the monks being served bleeding meat from a tarnished silver platter. "Those nabobs are feasting, but we're only good enough for pig feed . . . ?"

Hull's eyes roved the room for a way out when he caught Obregon staring at him. The bandit's blunt features were scoured into a red mask by the desert, his hawklike nose split almost in two by a grievous hatchet-wound, wiry thickets of beard pocked with scars; he was perhaps the second hardest thing to look at in this place. "What are you staring at, coyote?"

"Your wanted poster flatters you," Hull said.

To sit at table opposite men he'd been hunting would have been a puzzlement even in a less discouraging setting. Noticing the silent Mexican at the far end of the table, who stared at the corn with ravenous despair, he recalled what the disembodied voice in his cell had told him. *Eat nothing they give you—*

Hull felt as if he wore shackles and a ball and chain around his neck, but he watched over Obregon's shoulder as the server set the platter before Fray Joachim. Something about the server struck Hull as particularly wrong: his head was less than half the size it should be, and he was equal parts irked and relieved that the peaked hood hid it.

Fray Joachim took hold of a joint of meat, scorched with the same indifference as the corn, and began gobbling it down. The other monks sat stock-still with their waxen hands on the table before them, staring straight ahead in denial of the butchery piled before them. Their hoods hid all but the lower half of their scowling faces, but Hull noticed the fine markings around their dour mouths and began to suspect . . .

But why would their mouths be sewn shut?

Eight-Finger Nate let fly a raucous guffaw. "I do believe that's your horse they're eating, half-breed. Reckon you're entitled to a share. Why don't you go ask for it?"

Indeed, it was so. Fray Joachim devoured the meat with gusto, bones and all, while the others sat like statues.

"You're in the same soup as us, ugly," McKeever said, reaching for his cup, when lightning struck his mangled right hand. A vicious snap sounded almost after the bandit had recoiled from the clay cup, which shattered and spilt its pitiful mouthful of water on the table.

The wrong-headed servant stood behind McKeever with a knotted whip poised to strike again. His hood had fallen back far enough for Hull to see that his skull stopped at the bridge of its nose, a rude knot of skin stitched with leather thongs closing over a wound that should have killed anything walking. Hull had heard of freak chickens that lived on with their heads cut off, but the monk was something else again.

"Hold, Trinculo," Fray Joachim said in the same archaic Spanish as the ghost in his cell. "Let him repent, if he will."

Eight-Finger Nate was on his feet, his good hand at his side where he once had a gun. Once a fast trigger and handy at cracking safes, but after a fouled shotgun blew up in his hand he turned to banditry. "Tickle me again," he snarled, "and I'll bite off the rest of your head, see if I don't."

"If you will not eat," said the friar, "you will not drink."

The friar stood, reaching with one hand for the knot at the end of a thick rope that hung from a hole in the ceiling, while Trinculo shuffled quick as his crooked legs would take him from the dining hall.

He didn't have to ring the bell. Nate McKeever sank into his seat like a whipped dog. With his good hand he took a fistful of corn and filled his mouth. "This is no way to treat white men," he muttered, and Hull had to agree. But it was no better or worse than the Franciscan monks had treated Indians for centuries in this part of the country. They were enslaved and worked to death and worse, they were made to forsake their language, their land, their families, their faith, their world.

"I am good Catholic," Joaquin Obregon said. "My cousin took the vow. I have nothing to fear from these heretics, but you pagans . . ."

Hull took a fistful of corn from the bowl and mimed putting it in his mouth, palming it into the breast pocket of his patchwork cavalry tunic. He drained his cup, looking steadily at the friar, who stood watching the men. He noticed the Mexican abruptly bend down to catch the rivulets of water from McKeever's broken cup as they trickled to his end of the table. He caught them in his parched lips just as the bell tolled, and they all rose from their seats.

"You will see," Obregon whispered. "Our Lord and Savior will deliver me from this place."

"Save your breath." Licking his lips, the peasant found his voice at last. "None of us will be saved."

2

They left the dining hall by another door and followed Fray Joachim across a paved courtyard and into a chapel. If anything, it was darker within than without, though a single tapered candle guttered in the vestibule. Moving like clumsy puppets, the men shuffled past the friar into the musty darkness of the chapel. They fumbled through layers of heavy sailcloth curtains infested with dry-rot and moths; and when they had won through to the lightless cavern, they fumbled blindly for the pews and settled into them.

There was a rustling of heavy wool and a scuffling of leather sandals as the last leaden echoes of the bell dissolved in the air. Fray Joachim's voice came from the altar, the guttural drone so low and slow that it seemed to take a score of minutes for each syllable to pass his lips.

Hull sat and listened. With only the soreness of his seat to mark the time, his hearing grew ever more acute, though his eyes never adjusted to show him more than pure blackness. Fray Joachim chanted and other monks took up the chant from every corner of the chapel.

By and by he heard Obregon snoring. The whip cracked. Obregon barked, lurching to his feet, but he sagged back into his seat just as quickly, and soon Hull heard his dull voice added to the listless chorus.

Far as he could see, church was always just a place for folks to talk to themselves, and all the games and frippery that went with it just showed how hard it was for them to trust their own gut, without it being some sign from heaven. He knew from bitter experience that there were other ways to get the ear of the secret powers of this world, ways that would bring power at an unthinkable price. He chased his failing brain in circles trying to resist this thing they prayed to, for he knew that it was, unlike the god of the Franciscan missionaries, right here in the room with them, and it eagerly answered any prayer.

Hull felt the darkness close in and thicken. His eyes made phantasms out of the perfect darkness, purple writhing things like huge glow-worms swimming in tar. The chapel seemed to grow colder, the shadows to rasp against his hands and face like dead women's hair, like spiderwebs and scorpion legs, making him itch all over until he thought he would scream and flee, whip or no whip, bell or no bell. The urgency of it redoubled as the chanting grew louder and quicker, to resolve into words, into a word . . .

ZU-XE-QON.

Do not let the darkness into your mouth—

A thunderclap and lightning walked across his back. All his will fell short of lifting him to his feet. He heard the others and slowly, painfully raised his hands to cover his mouth as he added his voice to the chant. The itching became a prickling as if his limbs were starved for blood, the sensation of spiders with needles for feet walking all over him, converging on his mouth and kneading his flesh in their desperation to enter him. But he sat and chanted through his fists until the bell tolled again and the monks rose to their feet to guide them outside.

The moon was still high in the sky when they were led into the courtyard. The space was about a hundred feet on a side and surrounded by the cells on one side, the monks' cloister and a rectory on the other, with the chapel in the center. A high adobe wall blocked the fourth side, with a low door set into it that bore a primitive but formidable padlock. The top of the wall was twice a man's height and studded with obsidian shards.

Fray Joachim ordered them to tear up the cracked clay paving stones around the well and to till the soil. This part they should make haste to finish, he said, for the dawn was coming and the sun would not be so merciful as the Lord.

Fray Joachim and three more monks stood in the corners of the courtyard with their whips at the ready, but the shadow of the bell tower loomed across the courtyard in the moonlight filled him with dread down to the marrow. A crude flight of stairs climbed a corner of the chapel to the belfry. He saw the misshapen silhouette of Trinculo lurking in the belfry, polishing the bell and waiting.

"This is worse than any jail," McKeever growled under his breath. "Let's beat the shit out of these dog-dicks and hop that wall . . ."

Two whips cracked and split McKeever's shirt front and back. Blood splashed from the wounds, and for a moment McKeever looked fit to spring on his tormentors, but then he bent over and set to work.

All the rest of the night they worked feverishly under the whip, prying the stones out of the disintegrated mortar with their bare fingers. The ground underneath was sour, as if the earth itself was saturated with poison. It mercilessly tore their fingers and greedily drank up every drop of blood. The wounds from previous whippings reopened and wept and they seemed to weaken with every lost drop, every fresh wound.

By the time the sun peered over the red-tiled roof of the cloister, they had cleared nearly all the stones. Fray Joachim ordered Hull, Obregon, and the woodcutter to begin tilling the soil and planting seeds, while McKeever would clear the rest of the stones in the portion of the courtyard that lay in the shrinking shadow of the tower.

As Hull worked under the punishing sun, he noticed how the monks retreated into the shadows of the cloister. Though the men flagged in their efforts, they were slower to whip. Hull had seen more than a few men on display in pine boxes, and the brothers' features spoke of the same sunken vacancy and indifferent mortician's care. Then again, he'd seen a thing or two that wore the shape of a man but shunned daylight like poison, or burned at its touch. Fray Joachim and the monks seemed to mislike it far more than the men working in it.

But something else alarmed him even more. All about their feet tender shoots erupted from the bad soil like green flames. They seemed to grow even faster underfoot, where the sweat and blood nourished them. Hull watched in morbid fascination as they sprouted and unfurled tiny leaves in his shadow, as if feeding on his essence to grow as fast as he could plant them. By the time he had emptied his bag of corn kernels in the corner where McKeever worked feverishly to take up the last paving stones, the far side of the quadrangle was knee-deep in corn plants, already gravid with ripening ears sheathed in waxy purplish-green husks.

He was almost too numb with fatigue of think anything of it, and when a monk came round with a dipper to offer him a mouthful of water, he was almost stupid with gratitude to those who were working him to death.

To death—

No such mercy was on offer, he knew by now. They would work him until his body failed, but he would go nowhere. In the heat haze of the afternoon he fancied he saw more than three other workers in the quadrangle. Bronze-skinned men and women in loincloths, conquistadors in doublets and steel bonnets, raving, weeping men in cavalry blues, fortune-hunters who still believed they'd found El Dorado and were digging for gold. Long after death in this godforsaken place, they still toiled and chanted those terrible syllables, just as he would when he died here.

He would not die here.

His brain boiled in his skull. His tongue swelled to fill his mouth like a toad in a hole. Exhaustion made him swoon against the nearest wall, but he took another sip of water from the dipper when it came and finished his planting.

As the sun dipped behind the bell tower, the monks summoned them to harvest the corn. He could hear them as he picked them, an unwholesome rustling, and the roots squirmed to catch the last drops of sweat from his blistered brow.

Hull did not wonder at any of this, for it would not have surprised him to find he'd worked for days on end, the nights passing in the blink of an eye. Just before sundown the bell tolled in perfect sync with the pounding in his head. Three of them limped out of the rows of corn. The woodcutter collapsed and begged for water.

Fray Vigil, quickest with the whip and slowest with the water, poured the dipper in the thirsty soil at his feet and smiled as the dying man crawled to suck the mud into his mouth, then perished with his face pressed to the earth.

3

When next the bell rang, it was all he could do to keep his feet. He steeled himself for another meal. Fray Joachim led them into the dining hall and took his seat at the head of the long table. A platter of raw corn and a jug of water awaited them. The bell-ringer brought the monks a plate of ears of corn. Fray Joachim took them one by one and ate them, cobs and all. Hull took a mouthful of corn and chewed it throughout the meal, drinking his water and silently battling Obregon for the rest of the jug. McKeever sat staring straight ahead as he fisted the corn into his mouth like a pig on market day.

Obregon tapped on his hand, then let the jug go. Hull noticed that he'd been tapping the table beside his plate all along, and caught what it meant.

It was a bastard version of Morse code that cons used to pass messages through prison walls. Hull picked it up during an otherwise unedifying stretch in an Arizona territorial jail.

Madness, the bandit typed repeatedly, until Hull met his gaze, then looked away. *Together,* he tapped. *Escape.*

Eyeing the monks at their table, Hull nodded, then inclined his head toward McKeever.

Obregon scowled. He looked to have shed ten pounds since the day before.

McKeever grumbled under his breath as he ate and seemed unaware of his dinner companions. Obregon kicked him under the table and pointed outside, then a flurry of hand gestures.

McKeever nodded and started to say something, but only corn spilled out of his mouth. Obregon kicked him again just before they were led back to their cells.

Hull could not lie still until he knew he was alone, and then he fell into a shallow, fitful sleep. Waking with stomach cramps from hunger and thirst, he reached for the corn in his pocket, but couldn't find any. The thick woolen fabric of the empty pocket was riddled with tiny holes.

He heard the echo of laughter.

"What the hell is this place?" he demanded.

The bodiless voice, barely audible, seemed to echo his words. "Hell . . . is this place . . ."

Still faint, but somehow much closer, it said, "Listen." The word tickled his ear. Hull might have fallen asleep and dreamed what he heard, but his bones and belly would not let him rest, and no dream this side of opium could contain such folderol.

"Zu-Xe-Qon is the living darkness. His word is the worm.

"Listen, if you would live.

"They feed you the worms, and the worms gnaw all but bones and skin. Worms eat each other until a man is but one worm that walks. Lips are sealed and the last worm starves, eaten by darkness. Only when there is perfect darkness within you are you saved by Zu-Xe-Qon.

"Zu-Xe-Qon fell from the sky, and those who found it served its appetite. Aztecs wiped them out, for their customs were unholy even in the eyes of men who ate beating human hearts. But they all unknowing took Him to their capital, thinking him but a rod of precious black crystal.

"So it lay unheard and unworshipped among the hoard of Tenochtitlan until the Spaniards came and crushed the Mexica empire, yet one monk hearkened to the undying echo of the black crystal and was seduced by its promise of eternal life. He had only to take its darkness into himself . . . and spread its message.

"His word was anathema, his followers tortured and burned as heretics. He fled north and settled in the most hostile place he could find, where men would come only in their extremity and beg for water, food, and the absolution of darkness.

"We were wrong . . ."

Hull could almost see the hooded monk huddled in the corner of the cell in the dusky murk. Hull asked the monk his name, but the door opened and Fray Joachim stood with one hand on the butt of his whip, and the bell began to toll almost before the echo could whisper, *Demetrio . . .*

The quadrangle was now a thicket of dead cornstalks tall as a horse. The stench of a battlefield wafted off it on the wings of carrion birds that gorged themselves on the spoiled blood-corn, stepping over their poisoned mates to get at it.

The experience was exactly the same, a routine ironed into eternity and somehow safe and sane. Hull followed the other three around the quadrangle to the dining hall. He barely noticed that McKeever was silent for once or that he did not eat, though he grabbed fistfuls of corn and pressed them against the rawhide stitches sealing his mouth. The monks sat twitching in their straight chairs, their eyes alone showing that something inside them was still alive, and as hungry and helpless as they were.

He scarcely took notice of the woodcutter at the end of the table, staring longingly at the water. When Obregon was caught chewing a strip of leather from his boot instead of his ration of corn, Fray Vigil reached clean through him to lay the braided whip across the bandit's neck.

They ate in silence until the tolling call to worship.

They entered the chapel through the draperies to find their seats and sit as the chanting started, as the chill stole into the room and the darkness commenced to walk all over them.

It began to make sense.

Why cling to this feeble vehicle of meat, when the darkness

offered eternal life? What did he get out of knowing he would die in the blink of an eternal eye, when he could live forever without fear? Forsake the world outside, forever eating itself, and seek eternity. Accept the darkness into you, and fear nothing . . .

He found himself chanting, repeating the words with a fervor that drained his last reserves, but he didn't care. His fatigue, his hunger and thirst, had overcome his flagging memory of who he was before he came here. He could give himself to the darkness and never die, or he could hold on to the illusion that he was nothing but a vessel of flesh and perish, only to find himself working forever in this place anyway. He could yet choose his fate . . .

A hand fell on his shoulder. He twitched, reaching to grab it, when he felt the subtle, quick tapping.

BE LOUD.

Obregon was an accomplished sneak thief, but an even more legendary traitor, playing family and gang comrades like cards. In the bandit's position, would Hull not lam out any way he could and leave the poor bastards to their fate?

No. Leaving anyone here was a fate worse than death. He had to believe the Mexican felt similarly. Even if he had no love for Hull, he wouldn't desert his old compadre . . . would he?

McKeever rocked and squirmed in the pew, oblivious to the repeated strokes of the whip. They would use any excuse to spill blood now, before they went to work. Blood fed the corn that nourished the worm, which fattened on the man until it starved in darkness. McKeever had made a pig of himself, while Hull and Obregon had only mimed eating the corn. Hull was so weak with hunger that he could barely make himself stand, could barely raise his voice above a croak amid the murmur of the chanting monks.

"Had enough," he growled. "Reckon we ought to know what you got us praying to . . ." Hull leaned on the pew before him and overturned it, throwing Eight-Finger Nate out into the nave. Turning round in the darkness and ducking reflexively in anticipation of the whips, he kicked his pew back and made as much noise as he could to cover whatever Obregon might be doing.

"Be silent! Be seated!" Fray Joachim roared. The command seemed to drop a fifty-pound weight on his head, but he forced himself to blunder through the pews. A whip striped his back. Another coiled round his left leg and threw him to the flagstone floor. A harsh carpet of woven agave fibers lined the nave, and he grabbed hold of it as the monks clamored after him in the dark. Their hearing might be acute, but they seemed to see no better in the dark than anyone else.

Grabbing the whip around his leg to jerk its wielder off balance, Hull struck the flint he used to start campfires off the stone floor. In the flash of sparks, the room leapt into crystal clarity that burned into his eyeballs after it had returned to darkness.

The effect was electric. The light threw the room itself into a convulsion.

The dismal chapel was bereft of any Christian iconography, the towering crucifix stripped of its savior, only a pair of disembodied hands still nailed to the cross, but Hull took note of how the darkness retreated into the rafters and the crypts and particularly took shelter behind the crucifix, where its wiry, spiky membrane burned into lurid embers at the touch of light.

In the instant before the monks threw leather on him, Hull realized that the thing they worshipped did not live in the dark. It was *itself* the dark, alive and whip-smart and hungry for new avatars.

He let the light die out in the moment Fray Vigil whipped

him across the back, having seen what he needed to see. Wherever Lope Obregon was, he had somehow managed to slip out of the chapel. A ladder behind the altar led up to a chimney that could only be the bell tower.

Fray Vigil and Fray Joachim stood almost directly over him. The friar called for Trinculo to ring the bell.

Hull struck the flint again so that a spray of sparks alighted on the arid carpet. The whips bit into him with a relentless fury, flaying the skin from his back in strips and chunks. In a moment the bell would ring and order would prevail and he would return to work and die like the woodcutter, devour the corn and be devoured, and one day his husk would wield the whip himself. As choices went, it wasn't so bad, but he crawled and crawled and when the bell hadn't rung, he reached for the nearest curtain and ripped it down.

By the weak light streaming through the humble rose window, he saw why the bell wasn't ringing. The rope hanging from the bell tower was looped round the bellringer's neck, whom Fray Vigil seized and upon whose corpse he pulled to ring the bell, but all in vain.

Hull scrambled for the doors and threw himself against them, falling into the gray pre-dawn murk and miasma of the quadrangle. The light pouring into the chapel raised a shriek like dry ice on steel. The monks rushed outside and slammed the doors. Fray Vigil lashed out with his whip, wrapping it round Hull's neck and jerking him back toward the chapel. Fray Joachim foamed at the mouth, empty eyes overflowing with inhuman rage. "We offered you salvation, and you betrayed us! No punishment shall be spared the monster who embraces flesh and fire . . ."

Hull's vision went dim. He could barely fight back, barely see the lumbering shape that loomed behind Fray Joachim, until it fell upon him like a buffalo from a cliff.

"Is this your god, little man?" cried Lope Obregon as he smashed in Fray Vigil's head with a long black rod that glittered with a sickening luster as it shed blood.

Hull figured it had to be the clapper from the bell which produced their master's unbearable ringing voice, even as the darkness was the star-born god's body.

The monk's head split open down to the chin like overripe fruit, leathery skin parting to spill out a tangle of worms, or a single worm, coiled and folded and stuffed into the husk of the man it devoured long ago. The repulsive bundle spilled out of his broken face and writhed on the sand between his feet, even as he tried to throttle Hull with the whip.

Obregon kept beating him, ignoring Fray Joachim. The other monks howled through their stitches in the chapel as something unthinkable happened inside them. Hull struggled to loosen the whip round his neck, gagging on the first fiery breath to get down his windpipe.

The doors of the chapel flew open and a shrieking apparition sprang out into the quadrangle to fall upon Fray Vigil, bearing him to the ground. Eight-Finger Nate had ripped out his stitches and succumbed to his hunger. Pinning Fray Vigil with one knee across his chest, the bandit snatched up the tangle of worm and stuffed it into his lipless mouth, gobbling it down like a pie-eating contest.

Hull could only crawl away from the carnage, thinking of how to get free and where they might find their guns.

Obregon beat Fray Joachim's head out of any remote resemblance to a human face and then smashed the crystal rod against the wall of the chapel, scattering the shards among the blood-corn.

"We should go," Obregon said, then chuckled as the scope

of his understatement caught up with him.

McKeever crawled away from the unsatisfying repast wriggling out of Fray Vigil and fell upon the still active remains of Fray Joachim. When the pitch-black sanctity of the chapel had been desecrated, the living darkness fled into the only vessel left to it, the body of its friar.

In his ravenous fury, McKeever ripped Joachim's body open and opened his mouth to eat the darkness even as it spewed like smoke from the crevices and cavities in the padre's ravaged body. Nothing but skin and bone, literally, and the darkness, which yet seemed to fill McKeever's body and satisfy his burning appetite at last.

Hull only watched in morbid fascination, until McKeever seemed to get his fill of the darkness and noticed Hull scoping him. Whatever was behind those eyes now regarded him with a patience that had gnawed itself for eons, a greed that could not restrain itself from eating the whole wide world.

The thunderclap nearly struck Hull dead before the bullet in McKeever's head let in the daylight that evicted whatever had taken up residence in it. It took the rest of the bullets to make it lie down, all the spaces a shadow could hide perforated and exposed to the rosy dawn.

"He was a good man, for a gringo," Obregon said. He dropped Hull's gunbelt in the dust in front of him. The guns had been emptied of cartridges.

"So what now?"

"I will ride away on my horse," Obregon answered, "and you will chase me, try to get a bit of money for my hide. Won't you?"

"I won't come after you unless I see or hear of you again." He didn't need to say if he would come after him, any more than he needed to remind him they were perhaps a hundred miles from the nearest settlement, and there was nothing else to do.

Forked Tongue

Just before sunrise, an hour before Cazador was to be hanged, a man came to his cell. He had filled his rusty mess kit with urine for the priest he knew would hector and crow on behalf of their pale god. The Apache war chief set the kit down when he saw the rangy Comanche half-breed with his long black hair plaited in a glossy black rope that lay over the broad left shoulder of an old Cavalry scout's tunic.

Cazador dropped the mess kit and dug a shard of brick from his straw bedding. Sharpened into a crude dagger, it would take more than luck to kill the cunning half-breed with it. But to have the life of the man who captured him and sold him to the Arizona territorial marshals, he would give much, and he had nothing to lose.

"Cazador de Cabezas," said the bounty hunter. "'Hunter of heads.' The Mexicans feared you more than Mangas. What's your Apache name?"

Cazador sneered, but his chest swelled with pride. "My Mexican name is good enough for you." Though he had been beaten by three jailers and burned with a branding iron last night, he showed only the steely pride of the unbeaten warrior.

"*Uzh-na-ti-che,*" the bounty hunter said, perfectly croaking the difficult Apache name. He came closer to the bars. "Your name *will* be remembered, if that's what you were after. Your people will speak of you as the one who doomed them."

"*My* people were the Coyoteros of the White Mountain. We raided from Colorado to Mexico every season and knew no laws but our own. *My* people died when they settled for the sour land at San Carlos."

"They won't even have that, soon. You don't know what you did, do you?" There was no mockery in the half-breed's low, weary voice. His hands rolled a cigarette, but his piercing brown eyes pinned Cazador with the conviction of eleven elders. "I guess the courts don't have to explain their case at a hostile Indian's trial, do they? Your band killed everyone on that train and stole the Army payroll. Stagecoaches and stealing horses are more your line. Who put you up to it?"

Cazador laughed until something under his ribs seemed to burst. "Their war chief is dead. This land will never become one of their tame states. They will think twice before they—"

"They *always* think twice! That's why they always beat you. Even when you kill them, you serve them."

He turned away from the bars and let his voice drop to a whisper. "You've come to confuse me with circle talk. I don't know what you want . . ." *Draw him closer . . .* "Their greatest warrior is headless in Hell."

The bounty hunter came within reach of the bars. "One thing you should know about white chiefs . . . they *all* lie about their war records. Little white lies, they call them, even when they're big and black. Mortimer Babcock was the head of some kind of delegation sent out from Washington. Who told you he was a great warrior?"

Sharpened stone thirsty for blood, Cazador turned to face the bounty hunter, who leaned on the bars and offered Cazador the cigarette. With a good throwing knife he could cut the murderer's throat from across the cell.

"Who told you to take that train? Who gave you those new

Winchesters your braves had when they were all shot down at Agua Dulce?"

Cazador spat at the slur on the purity of his hatred. The bounty hunter set the cigarette on the bars, its sour smoke coiling up in a knot in the stifling heat.

"I had to ride you down and carry you back from the border, and I don't feel at all right about it."

"Give the money back."

"I'd rather earn it. Who paid you, Cazador?"

Slowly, as if walking on hot coals, Cazador came over to the bars. He snatched the tobacco and sucked it until his lungs filled with smoke, but he said nothing.

Reaching into a pocket, the bounty hunter produced a small bundle and began unwrapping it. "Your people said you wouldn't talk to me. But they said you might change your mind if you saw this . . ."

Cazador whispered a name under his smoky breath. The bounty hunter came closer to hear. Cazador caught his arm and jerked him off balance, slamming him into the bars. His other hand shot through the bars to stab the bounty hunter in the gut, but a faster hand trapped his and twisted two of his fingers until his hand went numb and lost the brick shard. Only then did he see the rattlesnake coiled round the half-breed's other hand.

Cazador released the arm with a high, hollow scream, but before he could retreat he was struck.

The fangs slid deep into the webbing of his right hand, scraping the bone. When he jerked back with a shrill scream, they seemed to break off in his flesh.

The bounty hunter clutched the big bull rattler by the back of its skull. Thick as a forearm, its scaly gray-brown body dangled down to the brick floor. It hissed and drooled bloody venom from broken fangs. A white crescent was painted on the flat crown of its skull, between its slitted golden eyes.

Fiery agony raged up his arm, so overwhelming that he had to bite back a hot rush of vomit. Cazador retreated to the far corner of his cell with his head spinning. He dug in the wounds for the fangs, but he couldn't find them. He could feel them in his blood, inching closer to his death with every beat of his heart.

"Black-blood! Two-tongued witch!" Cazador cursed. "You tracked me for the white devils, now you kill me with snake medicine . . ."

The bounty hunter dropped the snake and let it coil at his feet. "I haven't touched you. Listen to me, *Uzh-na-ti-che.* You can still save your band from a worse place than San Carlos . . ."

Cazador shouted for the guards. The bounty hunter spat in disgust and stormed out of the stockade. His jailers emptied a slop bucket at him through the bars and laughed at his agony. They couldn't see the snake, couldn't hear the seething rasp of its eight-chambered rattle.

He remembered almost nothing of the stories the toothless old ones shared of the Father of Snakes, but he knew he was doomed.

He could feel the venom racing through his body like a thief putting out all the lights to bring the Great Dark even as his skin began to burn with a furious itching that didn't abate until he was bleeding . . . an itch like the growth of new skin beneath a wound.

Please, he begged any spirit who might hear, *let them not wait an hour to hang me . . .*

There seemed little point in staying to watch them hang Cazador de Cabezas. But the bounty hunter lingered at the back of the crowd when the troopers marched the last true war chief of the Coyoteros out of the adobe stockade and up to the scaffold. Cazador made no statement as they hooded him and drew taut the noose.

Cazador was hooded with a dirty cotton sack, and a brief declaration of the pertinent facts was made by a scar-faced territorial agent who looked like a ranch manager. Then the lever was pulled. Uzh-na-ti-che, alias Cazador de Cabezas of the White Mountain Coyotero Apaches, dropped to his slow and agonizing end. If the drunken hangman had simply misjudged the drop and let Cazador strangle rather than fall to a clean death, then he should not have smiled so to watch him twitch and dance for over three minutes.

Finally the hangman, the agent, and the deputy marshal ambled down from the scaffolding, leaving the Apache to twist in the morning breeze. Children threw rocks at the corpse. Only then did Inigo Hull turn to leave.

Truly, it was no better than Cazador de Cabezas deserved. A ferocious killer of women and children, he was only less infamous than Mangas Colorados or Victorio because he lacked their head for strategy. Too hotheaded to run with any other chief for long, Cazador led his small splinter gang in messy, vicious raids from Colorado to the Gulf of California. The White Mountain Coyoteros were among the first bands to settle on the San Carlos reservation, but though they struggled to survive on bad rations and sad little ranches, they were all punished for the crimes of bad seeds like Cazador.

Still, it did nobody any good to let his corpse hang like a trophy in the middle of Fort Apache. Hull shouldered his rifle and shot the taut rope, heard the muted thud of the body hitting the hard sand beneath the gibbet.

A few infantrymen pointed their carbines at the mounted bounty hunter, but a sergeant who remembered Hull's service in the Indian Scouts told them to mind their own business.

Hull rode over to the trading post and found a couple of boys to put Cazador de Cabezas into a pinewood box. He shouldn't squander any part of the bounty on the Apache's remains, but something about the job felt spoiled. The territorial authority had paid well for Cazador's return, but with no bonus for bringing him in alive.

The territorial agent smirked at Hull as he came out of the telegraph office and climbed onto his horse. When his ill-fitting coat slid back from his hip, Hull was surprised to see a bullwhip on his belt, alongside a Colt Army revolver.

Hull had visited the San Carlos reservation to learn from Cazador's people who else he ran with, and they had given Hull something to show him. They had said it would loosen his tongue. Then the old medicine men had laughed until Hull rode away. Hull did not believe he ever wanted to hear an Apache laugh again.

Snake medicine.

Hull wiped his hand on his buckskin dungarees where it had touched the painted scroll of crumbling snakeskin. He still puzzled over the way Cazador had spooked when he saw it. He was fast and might have hurt Hull with his makeshift knife, if he hadn't balked just then, terrified.

Snakes were taboo for reasons that Hull had never been made to understand. The Apache would rather starve than eat turkeys or any other birds that might eat snakes. Superstitious fear at the back of it, but of what? Something far more powerful than a warning drove Cazador into a kind of shock when he saw the skin. And when he marched to the scaffold, had he not looked sicker than the fear of death would make a man, and holding his right hand in his left as if the arm were a dead thing?

Fool notions like this were how superstitions got started,

and how superstitions became religions.

After he bought some supplies and listened to a dry goods trader who'd come from Las Cruces through hostile Indian country, Hull stepped back outside and found two of the boys looking for him.

"Someone took it away," they said.

"Who took it?" Hull looked around, but saw no grave detail. "Where's your friend?"

They looked at each other, then back at the scaffold. "He's still looking for it," one boy said, then they both ran away.

He heard screaming from the livery stables. A red Appaloosa mare bolted from the barn with a rider clinging to the terrified beast's neck as it stampeded over a straggling line of infantrymen on the parade ground and out the gate into the open field.

A stable boy came out shouldering the boy Hull hired to put away the corpse. His face was swollen and colored like a bruise, and he was vomiting on himself. The stable boy dropped him and commenced rolling in the dirt himself, screaming that he was burning.

The red-faced Irish brute who ran the trading post came out onto the walk and whistled. "Reckon they're gonna want their bounty back, boyo."

Hull shook his head. "They got their money's worth. Reckon they'll have to pay me twice for the same neck." Still wiping his hand on his leg, he spurred his horse after the cloud of dust.

Immediately outside the gate, Hull reined in and pivoted, but the wind was drawing the Appaloosa's dust westward, down the river valley. The insane sonofabitch was riding south toward the Agency, plunging down the slope to vanish into the cottonwoods that crowded the banks of the Black River.

Hull rode out on the ridge overlooking the river until he was several hundred yards off, with a clear view of Cazador riding like hell for the crossing.

Squinting down the sight on the rifle, he waited patiently until the Appaloosa dove into the sluggish current and began madly paddling. He could make out the rider's long black hair hiding his face and the bloodstained gray of his shirt.

Hull had the Apache in his sights when his damned horse reared up under him. The shot went wild, the leaden roar of it echoing down the river valley. Hull tried to calm the yellow gelding. Wheeling and whinnying in utter unhinged terror, the horse had good cause to panic.

The ground all around them was rife with rattlesnakes. Braided tangles and writhing knots of young vipers boiling out of holes in the rocky soil. The rasping of their immature rattles was like a hundred beehives.

Hull snapped the reins and stood up in his stirrups to force the horse to run down the ridge toward the river, but the gelding's panic turned to agony as the snakes began to strike its legs. Singly and in rabid bunches, they clung to the horse's kicking, struggling legs. When Hull slapped the gelding's flank with the rifle stock, it lurched sideways and seemed to kick feebly to throw him out of the saddle.

Hull splayed out his arms and legs when he hit and rolled ass over teakettle down the rocky slope. He lay stunned on the ground, face up to the rising sun, for how long he did not know. When he got up, blood still flowed freely from a gash on his forehead. His horse lay dead amid the swarming rattlesnakes. He couldn't get to his saddle or his other gear, but it was a fair bet none of it would get stolen. Picking up the rifle, Hull stumbled down the slope to the reservation road where it joined with the wider river road that wound south around the agency about ninety miles to the provisional capitol in Tucson.

Dragging himself upright, Hull waved his hat at a cloud of dust that rose up from the road as if Cazador was returning with reinforcements. The dust parted to reveal a cavalry troop returning from patrol.

"D'you see an Apache on a red Appaloosa mare ride past you?" he shouted. The whole truth all at once would just slow things down. "Man they were fixing to hang escaped and was headed your way."

The second lieutenant scowled at the dusty, bleeding half-breed blocking his way. "We haven't encountered anyone until we nearly ran you down. We're just returning from a long wild goose chase, and are in no wise receptive to nonsense . . ."

"Please, Lieutenant. I need a horse to catch Cazador de Cabezas, and I doubt anyone else can keep up with him going cross-country. He's hell on a fast horse, and he's headed for population."

"I'll thank you to get the devil out of our way--" the lieutenant started, but his sergeant, a leathery mustachioed man old enough to be his uncle, climbed down from his horse and passed the reins to Hull. In the beetle-browed stare the man cast his way, Hull saw recognition and a grudging gratitude, and knew he must have served on the bad patrol when Hull saved the Sixth Cavalry from Mad Captain Ketrick and the Anasazi Circle Curse.

"Sergeant, I order you——"

"Beg pardon, sir, but I owe this man my life," the sergeant growled around a plug of tobacco, "and it's worth a damn sight more to me than a week in the stockade."

The fuming lieutenant looked to his men, who seemed powerfully preoccupied with the state of their tack just then.

"Much obliged," Hull said.

The sergeant cracked his idea of a smile. "Mighty partial to this horse."

"Have it back to you directly," Hull answered, swinging into the saddle and putting his heels to the horse's ribs to send it pelting down the road.

The high-pitched squall of the officer's tirade faded behind him fast. The horse was worn but well fed and watered, and she seemed to cotton right away to the urgency of the matter.

Riding down the slope on the road with his eyes on the uphill side, he covered less than a mile before he spotted a broken branch on a tree in the mouth of a steep canyon that shadowed the road, running mostly south until it played out at Natanes Plateau. It would be slower than the road, but he'd already dodged a patrol. He wasn't headed for the reservation, at least. But where the hell was he going?

Predicting Cazador's next move would be a lot simpler if he knew for certain whether the Apache was alive or not. Whatever the Coyotero elders gave him to show Cazador must have had something to do with it. Whether it allowed him somehow to play possum and ride out the hanging or if it made him too sick to die honestly, he couldn't say. Hull had seen dead men do all kinds of things they weren't meant to in his time, but he knew of nothing that would make a dead man rise up and ride like a devil.

Best to stick to what he did know. Cazador was an outcast even among Apache warriors because he couldn't let go of a grudge. Hull had been sure someone had put Cazador onto the train raid, and he was certain the Apache would want to see someone pay for leading him on. Cazador kept mum because he didn't know, or cursed himself for a fool and so couldn't reveal who had backed him.

Cazador lived for revenge. The Apaches believed revenge was central to honor. They would want to see whoever shamed their tribe pay with more than just his life, if they could. But if Cazador wanted vengeance, he had only to turn around and ambush Hull. He had caught the Apache alive, denying him a warrior's death, and brought him back to be hanged. His last act before he was hanged was to try stabbing Hull.

A sneaking suspicion grew and began to iron out Hull's tangled brains. For all he knew, it was Hull himself who kindled this when he told Cazador that the man he'd murdered had been no great white war chief. Whether or not he wanted to, whether or not he knew whom he was hunting, Cazador had been put on a warpath, and God help anyone who blundered into his way.

The trail ascended for nearly a mile before reaching a narrow notch between pillars of sandstone and granite. The sun had climbed over the mountain and shone full into the canyon, but Hull rode slower than even the rough terrain demanded, casting suspicious glances to and fro and even at the ground beneath his horse's hooves. By now, Cazador might not be alone. Geronimo was raiding pueblos in Mexico, Nana had regrouped after Victorio was slaughtered in Mexico, and no one knew where Mangas was. Plenty of impossible things had happened today, so the unlikely seemed almost inevitable.

Gaining the summit at last, Hull shaded his eyes and scanned the sharply descending mountainside. Nothing. He might have seen a plume of dust a few miles out on the open plain. Ranches and fenced grazing land began to crop up along the Gila. Rate Cazador was going, his horse would give out in a matter of hours. They were still about eighty miles from Tucson as the crow flew, and his own horse was lathered and panting.

He's only one unarmed Apache, his mind nagged at him. *He's no threat to anyone.* But Hull snapped the reins and drove the sorrel mare down the granite stepping-stones of the peak.

No ambush awaited him that he could see, but he felt as if he was riding against a tide of dread that threatened to pull his guts out to flap in the wind. It was almost as strong as the certainty that this whole mess was more than a little bit his fault.

Hull nursed the horse down the steep slope, but she gave out just after sundown. Hull staked her near a patch of grama grass and fed her his canteen of water, then set out on foot. He'd return for her tomorrow or send someone to collect her, if he was unable. He had no bedroll and, tired as he was, he couldn't sleep. He doubted Cazador would be making camp anywhere nearby.

Only an hour south, he found the red Appaloosa sprawled across the trail. He'd seen plenty of horses ridden to death by desperate men, but this was something else again. The mare's legs stood out stiff, and the head was contorted back as if the beast had tried to break its own neck in its convulsions. He almost touched it to see if it was still warm, but something made him draw his hand back as if from an unseen flame.

Its eyes were not right. The moon had not yet risen, but the stars afforded enough light to see that they had burst from their sockets. Its tongue had swelled to block its throat, and the lathery flesh on its unsaddled back was a bed of weeping ulcers the size of hen's eggs.

Hull stepped back, scanning the ground for any sign of rattlers, but the brush was silent, devoid of life. A few clumps of black turned out to be vultures—about six of them, dead as doornails with their gizzards spilled out from their beaks.

This horse wasn't just exhausted. It was pumped full of venom, and it was worst wherever Cazador de Cabezas had touched it.

Backing away from the grisly scene, he found Cazador had left an unmistakable trail. His tattered, bloodstained shirt hung from a yucca branch; his pants lay on a rock beside the trail; and further ahead he saw white, gauzy shreds flapping in the wind from the low branches and the boles of piñon pines. Running down the trail, Cazador seemed to have stripped and then shed his own skin.

Tired, parched, and spent as he was, Inigo Hull found the strength to run, at least until he was far from the horse's carcass.

As the sun came up, Hull limped into the dooryard of a ranch house. It was a small, hundred-acre spread with no fulltime hands, only the one family, and he saw nobody. Sick certainty told him he wouldn't, for they must all be in the house, which was on fire.

The barn stood open. The horses shrieked and kicked the walls of their stalls, nearly kicked his brains out when he set them free. He chose the least hysterical riding horse and led it out by a lariat. After trying to bolt and kick him a few times, the slate-gray bronco took a bridle and saddle and bore him on the road south.

Hull was ill at ease in any town with more than one street, and Tucson had almost a dozen. Since the territorial capitol was moved here only a decade before, the town had become a full-fledged city, with lawyers and politicians and other symptoms of civilization as thick in the streets as the bygone buffalo herds. Hull couldn't imagine the fugitive Apache could pass unnoticed in the town. He spotted two deputies on the steps of the capitol and a retinue of private guards escorting a carriage that parked before the capitol to a great stir among the lurkers on the sidewalk. The silver-haired but hale man who emerged from the carriage, Hull quickly gathered, must be John Anson Bowlund, the territorial governor. Another great war chief known for his bold campaigns to wipe out the Apache menace once and for all, waged with a pen from behind a desk.

Hull figured he should go see the sheriff and try to get in front of Cazador before he did whatever it was he'd come to do. He felt lost and out of sorts until he saw a familiar face in the crowd.

The scarred territorial agent handed his reins to a stable boy and went up the steps but deliberately bypassed the crowd of reporters and other petitioners around the governor. Pausing at the top of the steps with a calfskin valise under one arm, he sneered over his shoulder at the crowd for just a moment, long enough for Hull to think he'd been spotted. The scar that seamed his face from eyebrow to chin pulled down his right eyelid, making him look sleepy, slow.

Hull swung down from the gray and tied it to a post across the street from the territorial legislature hall. Making his way across the street, he went through the open front doors and stepped behind a column to survey the politicians preening in the atrium. The agent went through a door at the end of the hall. Hull slipped smoothly and quietly through the knots of talking gentlemen and cleared the door before the curiosity about his rough appearance touched off a small furor.

Hull found himself in a dim stairwell. Flattened against the wall, he heard footsteps going up and stealthily followed. The hall was three stories tall, with hearing rooms, clerk's offices, and a library above the room where the elected representatives for the counties into which the land had been carved up hatched their schemes to tame the last vestiges of Indian Arizona. He heard the agent's heavy boots climb to the top landing, and then heard a door open and close. Hull moved up to the next flight, but then froze when he saw movement on the landing. The agent had not left the stairwell, but had waited for someone else who came to meet him out of the public eye.

"Mr. Joyner, I have little time for—"

"Good news and bad, boss."

"On with it!"

"The Apache hanged yesterday morning like I said, but—"

"But what? He was a renegade, despised by his own tribe; you said as much. If there are more loose ends, sew them up. We've nothing to fear from the people of Arizona. When we become a state, they'll remember who settled the goddamned Indian question once and for all."

"But they sent another telegram right after, those idiots at Fort Apache. They said the Indian escaped on horseback."

"You said he was hanged!"

"I *saw* him hang, damn it. They've got their wires crossed. More likely, they just don't know one Indian from another."

"So he's *not* still at large? This only grows more confusing."

"No, I saw the right man hang. I'd know him, wouldn't I? He did you a bigger favor than any of your fatcat friends in Washington."

"I have no friends in Washington, but I won't need any, now. But this whole blamed mess . . . I can't be connected to it. If there's any trace, I'll—"

"You won't have to, boss. There was no hoopla back east, when Babcock came out. The President must've thought he'd spring it on you as a surprise."

"Backstabbing sonofabitch probably never figured I'd know he was sending that Indian-loving swine Babcock out here to take over. When they hear my speech today, they'll roll over and pretend they never cut the order."

Mr. Joyner gave a nasty little laugh. "Thought you'd like to have these for a keepsake."

"You imbecile, they should've been burned. Take them

away. Even if he is somehow out there . . . we have nothing to fear from one man, do we?"

"One man who burned down your enemies and put you in the catbird seat, who I watched dance on the end of a rope yesterday? Oh no, sir, I wouldn't worry overmuch."

"See to it just the same, Joyner. I've got history to make."

The door opened and slammed shut. Hull slowly began to descend, when a thunderclap filled the stairwell and white fire consumed his arm. His revolver fell from spasming fingers. His head spun as he tried to see what the hell had hit him. Lightning struck again and a coil of rawhide encircled his neck and yanked him off his feet and over the railing.

"Thought I smelled a coyote," Joyner said. Jerking the bull-whip, he strangled Hull from ten feet away and nearly sent him plummeting to his death.

Through pulsating purple spots that filled his sight, Hull seized the whip and yanked back. Joyner snapped the whip taut even as he came charging down the stairs with a bowie knife up to drive it through Hull's breastbone.

Still choking, Hull staggered on the steps. The knife came down just as he flung himself under and inside its lethal sweep. Driving his head into the bigger man's gut, he took all the falling weight onto his back, then pivoted and flung Joyner over the railing and down the stairwell.

Hull collapsed gagging onto the steps, prying the coiled bullwhip from his throat. He expected men to come pouring into the stairwell, but there must be a bigger noise somewhere else in the hall.

Working sensation painfully back into his arm, he likewise strained to get his head around what he'd heard.

This Babcock fellow was secretly picked by the president to replace the governor. The hangman had hooded Cazador before Joyner ascended the scaffold to read the charges.

It would be a good enough case for a lynch mob, but Hull had no idea how such things were done in marble halls with chandeliers and statues of famous liars everywhere.

Lurching down the stairs to the bottom, he found Mr. Joyner even heavier in death than he'd been in life. The calfskin valise lay on the floor beside him, its mouth yawning open to let the corners of a sheaf of bone parchment papers stick out.

Somehow his shock at the way white men ran things overcame his wonder at the black magic the Apache had wrought. *This is how they choose to run things,* he thought with disgusted wonderment.

Well, not today . . .

The Arizona territorial legislature had only just been called to order and made to stand for the entrance of Governor John Bowlund.

Though he appeared weighed down by a solemn burden, he wasted no time in mounting the podium and bellowing to the assembled representatives.

"Gentlemen, I come before you today not as the duly appointed executive of this great land that has given us all so much of its bounty, but as another outraged and frightened citizen, as one with the poorest among you, and sympathetic to the fears and anger of all our people. For while we have been engaged in the debate of the Indian question—namely, of the consolidation of our many scattered and poorly managed reservations into one great community in the verdant southwest corner of our state, which would provide for the greater good of the Apache and the security of all this territory's citizens— we have been continuously second-guessed by political interests clear across this great nation, who have seen fit to dictate how we should protect our homes and repay the incorrigible savagery of the hostile Apache nation within our borders.

"Only two scant weeks ago, another overseer was sent out from Washington to run our affairs for us, when he discovered the harsh realities of life—and death, I am sad to say—on the frontier. Killed by hostile Indian raiders while riding a train! It would seem to put the lie to any claims that order and felicity reign over all peoples in Arizona, or that the red man can be fully rehabilitated to join his white brothers in peace and harmony.

"A shameful blot upon our good name—until yesterday, when the last of the bloodthirsty band of killers who raided the train and slaughtered Mr. Babcock's delegation was hanged at Fort Apache, after having been apprehended by our good Arizona peace officers.

"The message sent back to Washington should be unmistakable. Order will not prevail in Arizona if it is to be governed from Washington. We, the citizen government of this territory, know how to settle the questions before us—"

The governor had them in the palm of his hand, those who were actually awake and sober. But his concentration wavered when a rain of paper came wafting down from the empty gallery at the back of the hall.

The governor sputtered and barked, but the spell was broken. A delegate grabbed a paper out of the air and studied it. Another one shouted, "This one's signed by the president!" Against the governor's strenuous commands, they began to compare pages.

Only the governor was looking up at the gallery when the other shoe dropped.

The body of Cort Joyner tumbled over the railing and fell to yank astonished screams from the assembled worthies below, only to jerk upright and swing from the bullwhip wrapped around his broken neck. His head sat askew on his shoulders, his drooping eyes seeming to glower accusingly at Governor Bowlund.

One of the few representatives not hiding under a desk demanded, "What's the meaning of this, John?"

"I have never—never seen this man ..." The governor's words came in halting fits and starts as he backed away from the podium and toward the door to his office suite at the back of the hall. "Have the marshals search that gallery! A murderous Apache renegade is somewhere nearby, it's the only—"

Hull broke through the cordon of deputies outside the hall and plunged down the aisle. "Governor Bowlund set up the Apache raid that killed a fellow the president picked to replace him."

"That's a damned lie! Arrest that man!" Governor Bowlund threw open the door to his office.

Hull was seized by two deputies and had to remind himself not to rough them up. Through the open door he glimpsed something rising up from behind Bowlund's desk, a shadow backlit by sunlight pouring in the open windows. Before the governor could utter a sound, the silhouette engulfed Bowlund and stopped his gurgling whimper of horror with its own mouth in a gruesome kiss.

The door slammed shut. Chaos reigned. An oily gentleman pounded a gavel and hollered for order, but the legislature had become an outraged mob that shoved the deputies aside and crushed itself against the bolted, barred door until it gave way.

None could identify the extravagantly dead Apache warrior who lay across the governor's desk, a deflated, desiccated effigy with its jaw dislocated and hanging by one hinge from the monstrous ruin of its face. A long gray duster covered its naked body, which bore no identifying marks besides the noose around its neck.

The governor leaned back in his overstuffed rawhide chair, stunned and a good deal heavier than when he'd left the podium only minutes before. His eyes stared through the august company of supporters and enemies united in confusion and horror. His hands clutched at his belly as if something he'd eaten had come back to haunt him.

Staring into the glassy eyes of the dead Indian on his desk, the governor seemed, for a change, totally at a loss for words. But then his lips parted and instead of a sound, there emerged no words . . . only a tongue.

Long and slender and black and forked, it vanished as quickly as it came. Bowlund's mouth sagged open, his jaw drooping to his chest and somehow coming off its hinges to allow a rattlesnake thicker than a strong man's bicep to slither up out of his throat. Its mottled brown scales were marked, just above its hooded golden eyes, with a white crescent.

Shock paralyzed the audience crowded into the office, but the territory's liberal stance upon the concealment of firearms meant that several men present shot the rattlesnake to bits before the entirety of its seven feet of length could pour out of the governor's body.

When answers were called for, it was discovered that the half-breed bounty hunter had used the confusion to take his leave. Many would later have cause to envy him, and none objected when a motion was introduced to the effect that the events of the day's legislative session be stricken from the record and any mixed or unmixed conversation.

A little white lie was the only way to preserve the dignity of that august governing body. Surely, they told themselves, that would be the end of that.

Black Wind

1

In the violet light and the soothing breeze of early dusk, the three Apache braves turned as if to whisper about the rider who sat astride a dappled bay beneath the twisted manzanita tree from which they hung by their necks.

The rider climbed down, eyes raking the ground, and approached the tree. It stood alone on the shoulder of the nameless black mountain, overlooking the gnarled maze of canyons that girded it like a moat.

The bodies were covered from head to toe with charcoal and painted with white and red symbols. The rider studied them for a long time, then scanned the ragged mountainside for signs of movement among the shattered postpile of boulders, like the scattered bones of a broken god.

The markings on their skins were not Apache, but he had seen them on petroglyphs carved by those who came before. The other marks on the bodies were not so mysterious, if one only asked who could do such a thing, and not why. The wounds were grievous overkill, mute mouths testifying to the anger of the men who did this.

Vigilante lynchings were still all too common in these parts, and Apaches never went gentle to the noose. One brave had been gutshot, and streamers of bowel twined like ivy round his dangling legs. His body bore the scooped-out pits of a point-blank shotgun up its backside, and was surely dead meat before they got a rope around it. The others were beaten and bound before hanging, but the whole affair had been rushed, the bodies not quite cold.

Beneath the tree, a fire circle spewed silver smoke, ringed by the prints of bare feet, where the braves engaged in a ritual dance when they were attacked. Tracks from shod horses and boots cut across the ridge and trampled the fire circle, and tobacco juice and a shattered whiskey bottle dotted the scene.

The men who did this had come to save a child. He could well understand their rage, but he had sworn an oath, and though his word as a half-breed bounty hunter was less than nothing in most folks' estimation, he had taken the oath just the same and would see it through.

Scanning the rocks again, Inigo Hull swung into the saddle and reined his horse up the narrow scar of a trail that clove the rubble-strewn flank of the black mountain. Looking up the trail, he noted three more plumes of gray smoke against the purple sunset.

He heard shooting.

2

The white woman in the blue gingham dress stood in the doorway with her arms crossed, cradling a rifle nearly as tall as she was.

"I know your husband is out, ma'am," Hull said. "I wanted to speak to you, if you'd do me the courtesy."

She didn't speak or move to let him in, but he saw over her shoulder into the blue shadows of the adobe and clapboard ranch house. Fine oak and mahogany furniture, battered and faded by the rude, raw sun, and all the dusty miles between here and Ohio. To have dragged it all out here, she must have thought this was going to be some kind of grand adventure.

Her nervous cornflower eyes flicked from his to the chipped china mug of coffee he held, tiny in his knurled copper paw. "If you were sent for to get my boy back, you're too late. We take care of our own out here. My husband and our neighbors have already gone out to search."

"I know that, ma'am. I'm only after a few details about the boy, so I'll know better, how to find him."

"Apaches took him. You may as well go back where you come from. My husband will bring him back."

"Folks in town say the boy was taken from your home at night, while you were both asleep."

She nodded. Her eyes and her guard slowly settled down, as they often did when a woman got over looking at Hull and started to listen. After a lady's initial fear wore itself out, she got to wondering how he'd come by all the scars on his face, or for whom all the bullets in his bandoliers were destined, or how he handled the pair of big coffin-handled knives on his belt. His weathered but gentle voice, so unlike the hardcase party from which it issued, indeed so unlike how any man talked, put them under a spell. Then she talked, and sometimes she listened.

"These braves stole in, got the boy, and got away clean." As he spoke, he watched the shadow of a hawk swoop across the yard and up the façade of the house. "Now, the house isn't all that large—don't take that wrong—but if he was taken against his will, I doubt but you'd hear some commotion. There's those folks in town who say the boy never quite fit into the picture—"

"People in town never tire of hearing themselves gossip," Mrs. Slattery replied. Someone had paid a handsome sum to teach her to speak proper English and enunciate the hell out of it.

"Well, ma'am, it's said he's prone to wander and to keep to himself, and when your husband has been drinking he's been heard to mistreat and even deny the boy, saying the seed in him died from the smallpox, so——"

Her eyes went flinty, all gained ground lost. "Who would ever hurl such slander?"

"Ma'am, I'm not here to point fingers. I'm here to find the boy before something happens that can't be taken back."

"You're not even half a white man, are you? No white man would ever say such things."

Hull looked off at the yellow horizon, at the distorting waves of heat rampaging across the land like shimmering, almost-visible beasts. His voice went real soft, but it cut right through her. "I'm half-Comanche, ma'am, but I don't see as how that would slow me down in finding your boy."

"I only meant that it's a hell of a thing to ask of the world to bear the weight of a half-breed who don't know his place." Her little chafed hands deftly cocked the rifle in her arms.

"No offense taken, Mrs. Slattery. Now, I won't trouble you no more . . ."

Hull shuffled off the porch and crossed the swept yard, his eyes all over the ground. "There's no place he might go, to keep to himself, to daydream, to hide out, to feel safe?"

"None of his things was taken, and he wouldn't have gone off in the night in his nightshirt. This is his home, Mr. Hull, and if Mr. Slattery were at home, he'd make you respect it."

"And the Indians still hold a grudge against Mr. Slattery for some grievance, ma'am? He's not an Indian fighter no more. The last Apaches are pacified since Geronimo laid down his gun."

"My husband rode with General Crook, sir, when they ran that bloodthirsty devil down, and he still rides, when they go on the warpath. He gave them plenty of cause to hate him, just making a safe place for decent folks to live."

He took in the kitchen porch, at the far end of the L-shaped ranch house–kindling at the door running low, and a high stack of nickel milk bottles by a reeking smokehouse shed, but no cows. "No doubt. Yes, ma'am, that was a hot, dry year." Hull stopped at the far edge of the yard, studying a low cairn of rocks at his feet. "Was Mr. Slattery off campaigning the year this well ran dry?"

Mrs. Slattery nodded, confused and evasive, but her mouth chattered away regardless, as it must when one's only companion is forever off hunting Indians or shearing sheep. "The water went sour, and we've had to buy tank water ever since."

"That was the year your house was blessed with young Robert as well, wasn't it?"

"We'd prayed for a child, but for years we had no luck, and then when Alonzo went away to fight the Spaniards in Cuba, God saw fit to bless us."

"I heard he's a fine boy, Mrs. Slattery. Born with a full head of black hair; that's good luck."

Mrs. Slattery flinched and put her hand over her womb as if he'd accused it. "Robert is a fine boy, and sensitive. He did everything he could to gain his father's good favor. He looks more like Alonzo than Alonzo does, himself; loves the land and the Lord like him . . ."

"But Mr. Slattery let those wagging tongues turn him against the boy, did he? Young Robert was so distraught, he took to going off by himself, and being reckless, he got those awful scratches on his skin."

Concern misted her eyes, and she forgot him. "So terrible, those scratches. How dare anyone suggest Alonzo could make those awful marks, like——"

"Like Indian pictures, ma'am?"

She caught herself talking to this half-breed bounty hunter as if he were a doctor or confessor, and her cheeks flushed. "If someone hired you to run down those red dogs who stole my boy, you better hurry. You'd better get off our land, now, Mr. Hull."

Hull nudged the pile of rocks that filled the old well. The cairn collapsed on itself and tumbled into the yawning hole beneath. The ground crumbled under Hull's boots, so he stepped back and turned to look at Mrs. Slattery.

A rank breath of perfumed rot wafted up out of the well. It recalled the unholy smell of a whorehouse in Carson City that had fallen prey to leprosy, and of all the Chinamen the townsfolk hanged in their panic. The hole gurgled like a hungry gullet.

Hull dropped a rock down the hole, cocking an ear for a sound he didn't expect to hear. "Funny, isn't it? Folks in town know a lot of nothing, but they know a little something in spite of themselves, if you listen."

Hull climbed into the saddle and rode away without another word, seeing in his mind the small prints from bare feet going to the well but not coming back, and the discarded nightshirt, plastered with black, viscous slime, balled up in the rocks.

3

The trail narrowed as it climbed the back of the mountain, but the stones underfoot were disturbingly regular hexagonal rocks, such as a more fanciful man might take for ancient paving stones. The rust-red earth bore only sparse scabs of sage and mesquite, deformed by some poison they drew up out of the ground. If the Devil ever ran out of room in Hell, Hull supposed, he could do worse than to send the damned back to New Mexico, as trees.

The sky darkened and the stars came out, glistening and bathing the trail in their beetling glow. Some of those stars seemed discontent merely to wink and gleam where a patient eye could navigate by them, but pulsed and swam across the sky, forming constellations he'd never seen before. And unless his eyes deceived him, they grew, every time he looked up.

The sheriff had sneered at magic, but Hull knew whites believed in whoppers the Indians would never have swallowed. They believed they could turn the land and tame it with the sacrifice of their sweat and others' blood, to break it like a crank-eyed mustang and make it give them all the things they longed for.

A stuttering scream of bullets chewing up rock rolled down the mountainside, and Hull reined his horse up a narrow ravine sheltered on three sides by granite boulders sundered by creeping, contorted cedars. Tying up the reins, he slid his Sharps buffalo rifle out of its scabbard and tasted the wind. A breeze blew, cold as the stars, reeking of gunpowder.

Scaling one of the boulders, he picked out a path and darted from rock to rock until he came to a peak overlooking the next fire.

Only one body lay there, and it wasn't an Apache. Cavalry gear dyed black, marbled with dust, but his hood had been pulled back to expose the slash that laid his throat open to the bone. Backing down the knoll, Hull almost tripped over the body of a brave with a bloody knife in his fist. His head was split like a melon; the vigilante's comrades must have emptied their guns into the corpse. Hot shells sparkled like fool's gold around Hull's boots.

From this vantage, he saw the other fires describe a winding spiral up the mountain to the summit. If they meant to hide from Slattery's posse, they couldn't have been more careless. The Apaches were stubborn about their old ways, but what did they hope for? To keep this land, with its springs running to black slime and freakish livestock and blighted crops; to die for this ground so red, as if soaked with ancient blood.

Hull was up and running with the next shots. Lungs burning, knees and elbows smashing into rocks where his hands held the rifle, he froze when a shot cracked the air from the other side of the rock he climbed.

He dropped back and slithered around the boulder. A painted Apache brave lay across the top of it and fired another round, pinning the posse down among the rocks around the fire ring. Another brave lay at the foot of the rock, shot clean through the head. Bullets ricocheted off the rocks all around him from five revolvers and a pair of rifles.

Even with hoods on, it was easy to spot Slattery. He shouted at the posse to outflank the brave, and howled slurs and curses with every wild shot.

Hull rubbed his eyes and stared into the dark, though the starbursts of muzzle flashes burned white holes into his sight. A brave stole into the open and sprinted to the fire ring. The nearest bunch of vigilantes spotted him and let fly. The brave crumpled, but something in his hand fell into the fire, which flared up a wicked green and sent a torrent of noxious, glowing smoke into the sky.

Hull flinched as similar explosions bloomed over the other fires, forming a luminous spiral of ghastly emerald light over the black mountain. The eerie smoke rose up and merged into a fitfully glowing mass that blotted out the moon, writhing on the chill wind like a snake in a noose.

A vigilante strayed too close to the fire circle and was engulfed in glowing smoke. He staggered out of it for a few steps, scoured clean to the bone and scattered like dice when he collapsed on the rocks. The posse hardly seemed to notice, so transfixed were they by the green glow.

Hull shinnied up between the rocks and crawled away from the wild volleys of gunfire. The posse, spooked by the renewed fires before and behind, fired blindly up and down the tortuous slope, but the lone Apache rifleman kept them pinned down.

Every instant Hull crawled up the mountain, his back itched, his brain twitched at the bullets caroming off the stones all around him. His lungs burned with every gasp of thin, frigid air. When he looked out and down, a swooning vertigo overtook him. He dug his fingers into crumbling granite until his head cleared. He'd nearly scaled this unremarkable little mountain in less than two hours, yet the surrounding land was a sea of murk miles below. The horizon was curved like the back of a great beast. Impossible . . .

A vigilante's shotgun barked twice more and left dead silence in its wake. Hull stood and ran to the edge of the mound of boulders that adorned the lesser peak.

The final ascent was a sheer cliff of eroded granite, but the peak was split by a narrow defile, just wide enough for Hull to walk with his pistols out. As the walls climbed and nearly closed over him, he crept in with one Navy revolver aimed ahead and one behind.

Icy wind sawed through the slit in the rock. Hull steeled his nerve against the fear of what lay beneath the mountain. *The wind below, the ones who stayed behind, and those who come down from the stars—*

And the boy.

At last the defile grew wider, though the walls above his head drew, if anything, even closer, so that only a hand's breadth of starry sky lit his path. The walls of the defile retreated to create low grottoes, the shadowy depths of which were pocked with pits of deeper darkness. Doors.

Here the trail ended in a wide circular courtyard. Fifty feet above, the walls gave way to a circle of starry sky. Hull steered well clear of the inky ribbon of smoke that spooled out of the fire pit in the center of the yard.

The floor of the pit was choked with spiked, bladed cacti—mescal agave, of a variety he'd never seen before. The black, waxy leaves bore wickedly curved thorns, and the flowers, even in the dim moonlight, were almost too red to look at.

This place was old when the Indians discovered it. For centuries it had been a sort of monastery, a retreat where a lone Apache magician, a skinwalker, lived and kept a vigil, as the Apache shamans told him. He shivered, for it meant the rest of what they said might be true as well.

His ears strained for any sound, but there was only the crackle of the fading fire. Of the boy and the surviving Apaches there was no sign. Hull, his night eyes spoiled by the dying glow of the agave embers, almost blundered into another pit.

It was a hexagonal hole bored out of the stone, with a ladder of wood and leather descending into it, like a kiva, where Anasazi medicine men traveled to the spirit realm to converse with gods and elementals, flung out of their bodies on the wings of peyote.

As he leaned closer, the ladder stirred and creaked. Behind him someone growled a curse and let fly a shot that ricocheted up the defile, sending his own companions shouting and ducking for cover. Hull marveled at their stupidity, and then his own, as he holstered a pistol. Clenching the other gun tight in his fist, he lowered himself to the brittle first rung on the ladder.

All this trouble over a boy; all this killing over a spread of miserable land.

It was almost as stupid as sticking one's nose into it for money.

Hull made plans and checked his rig so nothing jingled, and when the ladder had been still and no sounds had drifted up from the shaft for some time, he climbed down.

4

Sheriff Tub Collier riffled through his thin coxcomb of gray hairs as if he were counting them, or searching for just the right one to tug, as he met Hull's gaze. For his part, Hull was hard-pressed to stare down the sheriff for looking at the two-headed calf that loped by on the other side of the barbed wire fence.

Hull climbed down from his horse and approached the sheriff, who put one big white gator-skin boot up on the running board of his glossy black Ford, so his coat skinned back from the Colt single-action at his hip. Hull had seen a few of the machines, but never ridden in one. He supposed it was a fine lawman's rig, if every outlaw he chased drove one, too.

"Good afternoon, sir," barked the sheriff. "Indians ain't seein' visitors, today."

Hull felt ants walk across his face and wrinkled his nose, but came closer. "I mean to see some folks over the hill, Sheriff."

"I heard tell a bounty killer was sniffin' around town, but I didn't put stock in it. Wild West Show passed through about a month ago. Maybe you got lost? Or maybe you're lookin' for a place to retire."

"I'm looking for the one who took the boy."

"So are a lot of folks. Twenty braves busted out of the reservation. We've got it well in hand, though. They'll only lead us to the boy, and justice will be done. So you just mount up and vamoose now." Sheriff Collier took out a Bull Durham pouch and paper to roll a cigarette, but his eyes never left Hull. Under his pale gray duster, the bounty hunter's hands moved, and the sheriff reached for his gun when Hull brought out a pipe.

As he tamped down tobacco in the bowl, Hull asked, "Indian troubles? I could put it right for you."

"Don't that beat all." Collier's belly shook. "Any day now New Mexico's getting statehood, but we ain't so civilized yet, we don't know how to mete out justice. We take care of our own redskins out here, scout. A lot of our ol' boys served in the cavalry. We know how to handle Apaches."

"I reckon you do," Hull agreed, his face blank. "So you have no trouble?"

"Oh, there's always trouble." The sheriff's fingers deftly skinned the paper taut around the wad of tobacco, as nimble as the busy legs of a spider wrapping a paralyzed grub. "Couple times a year, when there's an eclipse or a meteor shower, they get their blood up. Everyone around these parts has had stock stolen or mutilated, just cut up for spite. What kind of savage kills cattle just to kill them?"

Hull, who'd seen fields of slaughtered buffalo massacred to starve the Sioux, said nothing.

"I'm no fool for superstitious hoodoos, but there's folks think them Apaches cursed this land, to turn it against us. I've had cattle give birth to monsters to shame that sport, over yonder." He pointed at the calf that paced along the fence beside them. Its extra head lolled and bobbed like a dead limb, but it browsed at the sere grass and tugged something out of the soil to chew. Hull stared until he realized the calf was eating a rattlesnake. Its other head caught the tail, and they fought over it.

"Wells dry up, soil goes sour, black shit that ain't oil comes bubblin' up out the ground, damned redskins go blood-simple at every full moon . . . but you bloom where you're planted, as they say. This is our land, and it ain't no wilderness. We ain't payin' no bounty on scalps."

At long last Collier sealed his robust cigarette and put it to his lips. He went for his matches, but froze as Hull's hands crawled up inside his coat again and dropped out in a flash of sunlight off silver that blinded the sheriff.

Hull feinted left and up against him, then ducked right and down as a peal of thunder rolled down the road.

"You son of a bitch! You shot me!" Sheriff Collier fell to his knees and pressed his left hand to the exit wound high on his right shoulder, while his crippled hand tugged, useless, at his Colt.

"With this?" Hull held up the silver lighter and flicked the wheel to light the sheriff's cigarette. "Your man up on the hill is jumpy."

"*Sheriff!* Daddy, you okay?" came a shrill cry from up in the rocks. "I think I got 'im!"

"Billy, you shit-brained fool! Stay down!"

Hull stood and threw his gun up, crouched in the shadow of the shiny motorcar. His face still itched where the nervy deputy's staring eye had crawled all over it.

"Slattery thinks someone else sired his boy." Hull crouched and spoke into the sheriff's ear.

"Go to hell," Collier wheezed. "My boy Billy's gonna plug you good."

"I reckon he'll try, if he's your son. Blood will tell, won't it?"

"You're a dead man, you half-breed bastard."

"Why does Slattery hate the Indians?"

"I told you, the Apaches been cutting on our stock. Slattery, he lost fifty head, when they gutted some of his sheep and stampeded a bunch more into the river. Then one come up the road next day, demanding—like a goddamned lord, he was— demanding to see the kills. Said he was a medicine man. Slattery, he was off hunting renegades in Mexico at the time, but folks always talk, and he got it out of his wife when he came back.

"We don't abide redskins coming round our womenfolk. Rapists and cannibals, payin' social calls to the houses they attack by night? So Slattery and some duly deputized peace officers went out to speak to the ol' devil, where he lived up there on that black mountain, and there ain't been no trouble from that party since. That's how we handle trouble."

"Sounds like you got it all sewn up, then. I'll just be on my way." Hull mounted and trotted up the road.

"You go on over there, mister! Them Apaches hate half-breeds worse than they hate us, an' that's no small store of hate! You go an' try to find Slattery's boy. An' when Slattery sends you to Hell——"

"They'll just send me back again." A glint of sunlight off metal winked at Hull from a stand of sage fifty yards up on his left. Hull drew and fired.

"Ow!" said the sagebrush. "Dang!"

Hull rode into Apache country.

5

The last traces of moonlight were swallowed up before he'd gone five rungs down the rickety ladder, and he lost count of how far he descended in pitch blackness.

Above, he heard the distorted echoes of the posse, but he

forced himself to climb down at a steady, cautious pace. Several of the rungs groaned and settled under his weight, and one snapped as the rotten leather thongs binding it gave way. At one point he set his boot down gratefully on solid stone, but when he turned to light a match he stepped off a tiny ledge into open space.

A little scream escaped before he could stifle it, as he threw himself out to brace against the opposite wall of the shaft and push his weight back against the foot of the ladder.

The shaft delved still deeper into the mountain, and by groping along the ledge he found another ladder that continued the descent. Hoping this one, at least, was the last, he swung onto it and climbed down faster.

A voice high above shouted, "I'll bet they're hiding down here!" Gravel and dust showered his hat brim, tickling his nose, so he pulled up his bandana to snuff a sneezing fit.

Looking up, he saw a tiny star wink orange and white at him at the distant apex of the shaft. Then the light swooped down toward him, growing much bigger and brighter, as one of the vigilantes cast it down.

Hull was stunned at the depth of the shaft, for he could make out only a hooded dot peering over the edge, but the torch fell fast. Hull slipped around to the reverse side of the ladder and hung by his hands, exposing only his knuckles, which were bronzed enough to blend with the knurled wood of the ladder.

The torch flew past him, flames snapping like crippled wings, and hit solid ground only fifty feet or so below.

"God damn, it goes halfway to Hell!" someone shouted, and the echoing click of a revolver's hammer only grew louder by the time it reached Hull's ears. "Slattery, I think there's someone down there . . ."

A growl that could only be Slattery replied, "Put that away you fool, my boy's down there!"

When someone alighted on the second ladder, blocking out the tiny motes of torchlight, Hull climbed down the reverse side, the cold sandstone wall pressing at his back. When his foot touched solid ground, he carefully slipped out from behind the ladder and around the guttering pool of light from the torch, and moved down a steeply descending passage that opened off the floor of the shaft.

The cave was wider than the narrow defile on the mountaintop, but Hull had to stoop so as not to bark his head on the smoke-blackened ceiling. He lit a match and moved forward, balancing his creeping terror of the black beyond its pitiful glow with the need to be out of sight before the posse caught up with him.

The tunnel wound around until Hull suspected it would circle and deliver him to the vigilantes, when he came out in a wide black space. Flashes of fire all around him, like the muzzle-flares of a thousand silent rifles, drove him to crouch, drop his match, and draw on the dark. But the lights died with his, and in the opaque purple void of his spoiled night vision he realized he'd startled himself with his reflection.

Thumbing the wheel on his silver lighter, he held it high and saw with wonder the garden of crystals all about him. As the warm, molten light seeped into them and lit the whole of the chamber, his heart faltered in his chest.

If the hidden cave-dwellings above were an ancient outpost to guard against invaders, then here lay the city they had protected.

Every wall of the enormous space was honeycombed with doors and windows, chiseled and shaped into terraces and palisades, causeways winding up the drooping walls to the stalactite-dripping roof, where hexagonal chambers dangled out over space, shaped by a mastery of stone of which the Anasazi's cliff-dwellings were only a crude imitation. And it was all glazed with a crystalline crust of mineral deposits, so the city glowed like the heart of a jewel.

In spite of himself, Hull was gripped by a deep, gnawing fear. The builders of this city were not the ancestors of the Indians, and it had fallen into ruin before there were any men at all. But their lingering imprint was still as real as the horde of distorted Hulls that stalked him from every mirrored wall.

It had always struck Hull funny how white men treated the earth. They ripped it apart in search of wealth and buried their dead in it to protect them from the hungry elements, and yet they thought of Hell as a place beneath their feet, a fiery gullet that craved the souls of sinners.

The Indians, at least, recognized that the earth was a living thing. Many believed that they had simply been birthed out of their Great Mother, the earth, and emerged from her womb into daylight. But there were those who remained behind, who turned their backs on the sun, whose memory the Indians had striven hard to erase. They called this shadowy domain K'n-yan, though it was a word that meant nothing to them, handed down from their ancestors with a warning never to dig too deeply in the earth—

Unruly sounds from the shaft announced the clumsy arrival of the posse, and Hull took shelter in a narrow doorway, peering about in the shifting murk of the approaching torches.

And then, when he had been very still for so long that mineral-saturated water dripping on his hat had begun the process of sealing him into the crystalline ruin, he felt a stirring of the air on his cheek.

Warm and fragrant, with all the scents of the desert, and

the forest and the ocean as well, it washed over him and lured him deeper into the ruin.

He passed through catacombs lined with heaps of ash and human skeletons in low, narrow niches, but stopped before a body lying in his path.

It was many years dead, though the gray parchment of skin still clung to the bones. A loop of hemp wound round and cut into the twisted twig of the neck. Hull's eyes crawled up the dry cadaver to its skull, which had been sawed through, and the cap laid aside, like the brimless hats the Levantines wore. The exposed bowl of the skull still contained some morsels of black jelly, but the corrupted mess had been scooped out. An instrument of stone stuck out of the ghastly bowl, which Hull discovered with a shudder was a spoon.

The pieces came together, even if understanding brought no comfort. The corpse was surely the medicine man who'd come to Slattery's ranch to see the mutilated sheep. The last in a long line of spiritual guardians of the black mountain, the medicine man must have carried a lot of secrets around in his head. Someone had taken the most blunt and direct possible route to getting them back out.

Hurrying from this scene, he almost trotted through the crypts, desperate for the kiss of fresh air that somehow wafted up from below. Somehow there had to be a chimney that opened on the sky at the heart of the mountain. There would be the sacred place. There he would find the boy.

He stopped and heard the clomping and violent disturbance of the posse almost at his heels, and broke into a run, shielding his lighter, half sliding down the ever-steeper slope of the cave that plunged down as the air grew warmer and sweeter, with the promise of the wide-open sage, and the sea—

He stumbled out of the tunnel and emerged into another

open space. He froze in awe, thunderstruck. The spent lighter sputtered and died in his trembling hand, but the light was no longer needed.

The vaulted ceiling rose to join a chimney like the throat of a dormant volcano. The curious yellow eye of the moon stared down the shaft and bathed the cavern in its dubious light. A wash of chill night wind swept down from the stars and merged with the infernally rich earthly perfume that came from somewhere far below.

A dying fire guttered in a circle of skull-shaped stones on a wide ledge overlooking the deeper darkness at the heart of the mountain.

Hull stood for a moment in the relative brightness of the fire and the moonlight, but a rolling vibration that stirred the soles of his feet dared him to go deeper into the cavern.

He stopped on the crumbling lip of a black gulf. His fire-dimmed sight could see neither the bottom nor the far wall of the pit, but a flash of a pale form struck out of the dimness. A human form, beckoning to him . . . Hull glared out at the dark, and as his eyes adjusted, his hands went for his guns, though they could do nothing for him.

A body knelt on a lone spur of rock that jutted up out of the gaping cataract. He was painted in the black and white markings that he'd seen on the Apaches, yet he could tell by the size and posture that it was the Slattery boy.

Hull whispered, "You, boy!" as loudly as he dared, but the boy was frozen on the rock, staring down into the pit. Hull stared also and saw that it was not empty.

He wished for darkness, or blindness, to take away the sight of what filled the immeasurable depths. A squirming, churning maelstrom of viscous black ooze swirled round and round the boy's tiny island of rock. No stepping-stones, no boat, no sign of how he came to be out there, let alone how Hull could reach him.

The furious whirlpool churned round the pit like a tornado of liquid flesh, yet only the slopping slap of it against the islet in the center made any sound, for the walls of the pit were worn smooth as glass. Hull remembered the Slatterys' well, and what the sheriff said about tarry slime that wasn't oil, and thought of the two-headed calf.

The Black Wind.

Hull's pounding heart nearly jumped out of his mouth at the echoing blast from a shotgun, though the sound was so familiar compared to everything he saw that it was almost welcome. At his back he heard an answering downpour of shattered stalactites from the roof of the enormous cavern, and the startled cries of the men in the posse as they charged out of the ruin. At their point a black-clad figure dashed to the edge, all elbows and knees and gun barrels, shouting, "Hold on, boy, I'm coming!"

With no cover in sight, Hull crawled away from the edge of the black cataract until a bullet caromed off the floor just shy of his face.

"Lie still, devil," said a big man with a black bandana over his face, "and call your friends to fetch Lonny's boy hither." He closed in on Hull with a Winchester at his shoulder. Silently, Hull cursed the stupefaction that left him such easy pickings. He was going to die at the hands of idiots, and he hadn't done the boy much good, either.

But none of the vigilantes was looking at him now. They all were screaming as they looked up.

Hull snaked his hand up his sleeve for a short throwing knife strapped to his wrist, but then he, too, could only look up at the mouth of the chimney, as the feeble starlight was blotted out, and a buzzing horde poured in.

6

Long after noon, the sweltering heat and roiling dust devils blurred the lines of the Mescalero Agency where it sprawled in the elbow of the little valley, but there was no profit in seeing it clearly. The sun and wind had beat all but the ghost of the last coat of white paint off the clapboard schoolhouse, and the rows of ugly little cabins in defeated ranks beyond looked like so much driftwood at the bottom of an arroyo.

No man ever got less from his gods than the Apache got from theirs, but none ever fought harder for it. They called their god Killer of Enemies. The word "Apache" was not their own name, but a Zuni word for "enemy." If there was a joke there, it surely would not be lost on the ones who lived here. The White Mountain Apache were the sons and daughters of Santana and Cadete, who chose to sue for peace and were the first to settle for the reservation.

Hull rode past the agency headquarters without seeing the station agent or a single white face. A pack of children dogged his steps, yipping like coyotes and trying to spook his horse.

He saw curious silhouettes in the unglazed windows of the cabins, shapes darting between the schoolhouse and the stables—feathers, braids, dull gray metal. No young men or old ones showed themselves, and Hull took this for a bad sign.

At the head of the row of cabins, he stopped and threw back his serape, unbuckled his gunbelt, and slung it over the pommel of his saddle.

They came up out of every scrap of shadow on the street, rifles and antique cavalry sabers and bows drawn back, all trained on him. Hull looked around and took a deep breath that was somehow cold.

There was not an able brave in the bunch. Women, old folk,

kids, armless, legless, blind men. More than a few of them passed around nickel milk jugs. He suspected they were not filled with milk.

Hull could fit all the Mescalero words he knew on the back of his hand, but he caught the words for *kill* and *bury* among their whispers.

"The Old Ones," he said in Apache, as he'd been taught.

And like that, they took him to see them.

They led him to a bald sandstone ridge overlooking the reservation, and pointed to a hole in the sun-roasted shade of a cottonwood tree. Two small boys sat on a rock beside it with carbines longer than they were tall.

The Apache did not dig in the earth—not to plant corn, not for gold, not even to bury their dead. It was a sin, the last relic of a forgotten, ancestral fear. For the old men of the tribe to sit in a hole in the earth, strange days must indeed be afoot. Hull gave his reins to one of the boys and climbed down the ladder.

It was even hotter underground. Bitter smoke stung his eyes and blinded him with whorls of brilliant color. Fumbling, he crept along the rough-hewn wall of the hole to where it widened out, and a guttural hiss drowned out all other sounds. He froze as his eyes adjusted, listening for someone or something.

Presently he could see the sunken shapes of nine ancient men sitting around a fire pit filled with smoldering black agave blades. The fire pit had no bottom. The sound came from a black wooden box like an altar, with copper wires trailing from it and going down the hole in the fire pit. The elders looked expectantly at Hull for a minute before one said, "You ruin it by coming here."

"Ruin what?" Hull asked, and creaking fingers pointed at his feet. He looked down and saw the copper wire under his boot. The wooden box squawked.

One of the elders bent the wire so it gave the hissing noise again, then turned it off and pulled the wire out of the hole.

"I'm looking for the boy," Hull said, "and I'm hard to stop."

"Not here," the elder replied. "Gone home."

"I've been there. Where have all your braves gone?"

The one who spoke looked around, and another of the nine took up the answer. They passed the conversation around, so Hull never got to work any one of them eye to eye. "To Sierra Negro. To light the way for the Outsiders."

"They'll all be killed."

A third elder snorted and fed green wood into the smoke. "And so will you, if you go up the black mountain. This is the business of earth and sky."

"Slattery hanged an Apache who talked to his wife once. That's what this is about?"

"He has a blood-debt to pay, but that one he hanged was no Apache. It was a skinwalker."

Hull misliked the name, and all it meant. He waited for the elders to add to it.

"The white man is not looking for the boy. He hunts the true father of the boy." The elders rattled with tired mirth. "He may as well try to hang the wind that blows below the ground."

"His men and yours lock horns, there'll be more war than your kids and cripples out there can handle."

"We have lost the taste for revenge, half-man. The way must be lit. This was old when the Apache came to be; it was the way of the people who came before the people. Listen."

The oldest and most withered of the nine took a deep draught of the smoke and, without exhaling or coughing, croaked out his tale.

"The first men were born out of the womb of the earth, where the Black Wind flows, shaping the first things and all that came after. The Creator sleeps, but the Black Wind blows out from the womb to make new children—to eat the People, or to save them.

"The People Who Came Before were born under the sun and sky, but went back into the earth to live, in K'n-yan. They worshipped the Black Wind, which they called Ubbo-Sathla, the Unbegotten, and Its favorite children, the monsters that enslaved and preyed upon the People until the Twins killed them and led the people into the sun.

"But sometimes the monsters wore the skins of men. When the Unseen Empire of K'n-yan turned away from Ubbo-Sathla, they fell into true darkness, but the Black Wind blew still through the women of the People, and the skinwalkers lived alone on the black mountain."

"And now you worship this god?"

"No, but we fear It, for It is real. When a skinwalker is born to the People, he is turned out into the desert for the earth to raise. The skinwalker speaks for earth against the sky."

"Come again?"

"The Outsiders, who walk among the stars. They covet the bounty of the earth and would harvest it as the white men do. The skinwalker must dance to show them why the earth must go on."

"Twelve years ago Slattery hanged the skinwalker, so now the skinwalker's taken his boy?"

The elders snorted and looked around at the walls of the kiva as if they saw something glorious. "Your blood is tainted with the stain of the white man, so you cannot understand."

The nearest elder leaned forward and passed Hull a scrap of paper that, in the dark, looked to be a crude drawing of a spiderweb. "Remember what you swore," the old man said.

Hull bowed and backed out, climbing up the ladder into

blazing daylight and blessed wind.

At a whistle, his horse trotted to him and stood still to be mounted. As he passed through the agency at a fast canter, the women and children sulked at chores, while cripples lay about as if drunk.

No armed escort saw him out this time, and he wondered at the transformation until he saw a squat, mustachioed party in a white hat that strove too hard to make up for its owner's lack of stature. Two dusty scouts sat astride their horses, cowing the tribe with their hard eyes and rifles, as the little man dismounted.

"Just who in hell are you?" shouted the white hat, proving that if he wasn't the superintendent, he sure thought he ought to be.

Hull reined to a walk and tipped his hat to the super. "I was looking for my grandfather, but he doesn't live here."

"Now, you come back here—" the super barked, but an engine roared to life in the stables, and a fine red automobile screamed out onto the dusty washboard road.

The super howled, and the scouts took off after the car. Hull rode off in the other direction as the super struggled to get back on his horse. He looked at the sun and then at the crumpled drawing, and saw that it was not a drawing at all, but a map.

7

The air shook itself to bits. The rising fury of the infernal buzzing felt like a tuning fork ringing his skull. The vigilantes seemed to like it even less, and retreated to the corners of the cavern to empty their guns up the chimney.

Slattery wasn't a big or a formidable man, as Hull had come to expect. He was thin and reedy, the kind of man you'd pick up and use as a stick to beat down another man. But his eyes blazed with the fire of the fanatic, a torch to lead lesser men, but only down paths of frenzy and bloodshed. That light guttered and was snuffed out now by pure animal terror, and the effect on the posse was electric.

From where Hull crouched on the ledge overlooking the cataract, it looked as if they had gone insane. Only he and Slattery noticed the boy.

Slattery went to the edge and called out, "Boy! I come to fetch you home! This heathen witchcraft ain't no part of you!"

Robert Slattery turned at his father's voice and started to come to him, taking a step off the edge of the island of black rock jutting out of the noisome whirlpool. Slattery shouted a wordless warning, but the flood seemed to subside and shrink away, laying bare a narrow jetty down which the boy walked, slowly, laying a measuring stare upon his father.

"What've you monsters done to my boy?" Slattery rolled his eyes and went for his guns as his son came closer. Robert's narrow chest was daubed with black and white pigment, but it only heightened the relief of the raised scars all over his torso.

Throwing out his arms, Slattery went to embrace his son.

Hull turned and skulked away to where the rest of the vigilance posse had dug in and commenced trying to shoot down the sky. When he saw what they were shooting at, Hull was sorely fixed to join them.

He could never say, in a word, what he saw. They moved too fast, and it burned his eyes to look directly at them, as if the light didn't quite know what to do with them. He thought of insects, though they were larger than a man, and their wings, like nothing that ever flew over the earth, splayed out to fan the walls of the chimney. What they used for heads reminded him of molds and brain fungus that festered in deep, dark forests. They throbbed and crackled with the fitful glow of a vile, darksome energy, and the incessant buzzing was the alien, yet horribly intelligent voice of a hive.

It was this last that drove Hull to want to crush them, an instinct older than all living races, to destroy and erase them. Drawing his heavy black Navy revolvers, he crept into the deeper shadows along the wall, and watched.

Like a swarm of gigantic bats, the horde swooped down to flit and hover over the cavern floor. A vigilante with a rifle popped up from behind a low boulder and sprayed the closest of them until his gun clicked empty.

The bullets had as hard a time passing through it as Hull's eyes had taking it in, but the creature seized up, disgorged a gusher of colorless fluid, and crashed to the cavern floor.

Its fellows circled round it and busily unfurled their segmented limbs, like a mad surgeon's butchery kit. As he watched, Hull realized that the creatures wielded weapons that he'd mistaken for limbs, for they were as impossible to comprehend as their makers.

Their purpose was clear enough, when they spat ball lightning at the shooter. The vigilante shrieked and jerked out a spastic dance, cremated before he hit the ground. His comrades opened fire, but the shooting died away almost before it began, the men stunned to silence as the echoes of a shrill, piercing cry stayed their hands.

"Stop! All of you!"

Robert Slattery stepped into the middle ground between the invaders and the men who had come to rescue him. Not quite twelve yet, and nearly as tall as his erstwhile Pa. No wonder folks talked.

The boy was naked but for the black and white paint, and rivulets of blood from fresh scars. Hull marveled at them. The unspeakable sacred pictures he'd seen carved in ancient stones were etched into the boy's flesh.

The boy threw his arms up in surrender, but arrested and paralyzed each man, eye to eye, in his turn. "Who among you knows the business of earth and sky? Who would speak for all flesh to the Outsiders?"

"Get down, boy!" they shouted, and harsher things, but Slattery strode up with his pistols out. The things from the sky, no easier to see standing still than when they flew, tended to their machines. Their pulpy, convoluted heads changed colors and seemed to throw off arcs like lightning and mushroom spores at each other, working things out. Forgotten at their feet, their fallen comrade melted into the floor.

"You ain't no flesh of mine!" Slattery roared at the boy, and aimed.

"No, Lonny!" someone shouted over the sound of a single shot.

As one, the alien things twitched and came to life, blurs of antennae and claws and whirring wings taking to the air.

Slattery reeled and let fly shrill curses as his pistol dropped from his mangled hand. His red-rimmed eyes rolled over his hysterical posse and the maddening sight of the creatures from beyond the sky, but he could not bear to look on his son, for whom he'd painted this damnable mountain in blood.

Hull came out of the shadows, a gray ribbon of smoke drooling from the barrel of his pistol.

The shooting started again, but the boy stood in the crossfire, looking down at his chest. The old and the fresh scars in his flesh took on a new life as a pattern, a picture, revealed itself.

He'd carved a zoo into his skin: seas of eyes, horns, feathers, and fur, and a mouth that gaped from hip to hip and enclosed a forest of teeth. Now the myriad of misbegotten features spilling down from his neck to his groin began to bleed.

Alonzo Slattery stood his ground, all the bottled anger in him bursting out of his eyes and his mouth in wounded gasps. His shattered hand floated before him as if he hung from it. He lifted not a finger as his son turned to face him with big round eyes like he was seeing the whole world all at once. When the boy's scars all opened up and screamed, he seemed to sit down and go to sleep.

The wounds bled and tore open until the mouth showed its fangs and spoke. What it said, only Alonzo Slattery heard, but it sent him to his knees.

Hull stepped back.

The last straggling vigilante fired wildly into the swarm and tried to run for the tunnel to the ruined city, but a flurry of shimmering wings swooped down and rode him face first into the sandstone floor, whining tools already setting to work on the body. With a tube that squealed and bled a cold blue beam like frozen moonlight, they cored out the screaming man's eye sockets and ears, cut out his tongue, and hauled wads of gray tissue out through his sinuses, hollowing out his skull.

The fruits of this ghoulish harvest were deposited in canisters, and it moved on to harvest the rest of the vigilantes.

Hull took aim, haunted by the memory of the mutilated sheep . . . but then he thought of the mangled Apache bodies hanging by the fire, and his gun dropped. Fair was fair.

The bodies disposed of, the flying creatures surrounded Robert Slattery. By what luck or skill he had escaped the slaughter, Hull neither knew nor cared. He waited for them to come closer to the boy, but the still figure only drew into itself and seemed to sway. Freshets of blood sprayed from the gaping wounds all over his body. And things came out.

The boy took a step, and his legs swelled and split like stockings, wriggling pseudopods bursting out and carrying the boy along in a slithering, sidewinder's gait around the circle of winged monsters. As they watched, their heads pulsed like telegraphs. Colors that made him sick shaded into others too beautiful to bear, and he knew they would miss the point of it all, scared stupid as they were of this boy.

Robert Slattery's body tore itself open and disgorged plated scissor-blades like a mantis's claws, fins, wings, and paws and eyes and antennae and organs and forms Hull could put no name to. Its liquid limbs lashed out at one or another of the creatures as it passed, in empty ceremonial blows that demonstrated its might and the depth of its contempt for these intruders from the stars.

Hull watched as long as he dared, but the riot of animal metamorphoses grew too weird and violent for him to take in, and the sorry sight of the only human part left grew too heavy to look on any longer.

The boy's face was wracked with fever and strain and horror at what his body had become, at what awful knowledge awakened in him now, the stolen wisdom of that ghastly tomb-feast, which instinct had driven him to devour. He knew what the world really was, had seen the true face of nature, and was charged with pleading its case before the reavers of the sky.

Suddenly Robert's body shot a long sticky tongue like a toad's out of the gaping mouth in his belly. It lassoed one of the paralyzed flying horrors and yanked it clean off its many segmented legs, dragged it headlong into gnashing, raving jaws, teeth crunching through thorny exoskeleton and soft, pulsing fungus-flesh and gulping it down, impossibly, into some bottomless gullet in the frail body of the helpless boy.

Hull had seen enough. Backing away, he circled to where Alonzo Slattery lay on his side, looking down into the whirling black cataract. The vigilante raged at Hull and kicked him away. "Look, you half-breed bastard! Look what they done to my boy!"

Hull twisted Slattery's wounded hand to lever him back to the ground. "He was never yours, just as this land was never yours. He belongs to the land," he added, turning the weeping man to face the black wind, "and *that* is his father."

Slattery's last strings were cut. He slumped against Hull, who scooped him up. The limp body tensed and turned against him when the gun in Slattery's other hand went off.

Robert Slattery stumbled and fell down, a brushfire of scales and fur and flowers chasing down his flanks and blood spurting from his mouth.

From the cataract, at last, came a sound—

A black wave broke over the lip of the pit. Bristling with accusing eyes and foaming, furious mouths, it reared up to the roof of the cavern, then crashed down and flowed across the floor, sweeping up corpses and scurrying invaders with plain, ill-mannered eagerness. The Outsiders struggled to get aloft, but the churning torrent plucked them from the air and swallowed them. It was no blind flood, but a cunning, driven, living force, roaring with rage and hunger and lust as it came.

Hull threw Slattery across his back and ran for the tunnel. He shot at anything that stood up to him in his dead dash, but it was like shooting the sea. He holstered his empty guns and unsheathed the twin bowie knives on his belt.

The broad, coffin-handled blades of dull gray metal emitted a blue, trailing glow and made the air scream as they hacked through the flailing hailstorm of vengeful protoplasm.

Faster than any eye could follow, Hull dodged and ducked

and slashed through flying snares of devious slime, with Slattery howling all the while in his ear. The rampaging molten flesh shriveled sizzling away from the relentless onslaught of whirling, slashing knives.

With the black tide lapping at his heels, Hull stumbled panting into the narrow cavity that opened on the crypts. He leaped over the ravaged skinwalker carcass and seemed to pass over some barrier that the Black Wind could not pass, for it drew itself up with an anguished cry and ebbed back into the dark.

Hull dropped Slattery, but the man needed no pushing to get moving. He staggered along and made do climbing the ladder one-handed, wheezing and sobbing to himself, but finally reaching the top.

When Hull climbed out after Slattery, he found the man trying to run down the defile that split the summit, bouncing off the walls in blind panic. Hull followed him, but drew his guns. The things from the sky had been swept away by the black wind, but there would always be more; they must always have been out there, waiting—

Slattery spilled out into the open and collapsed kissing the dust. Hull came up behind him and gave a whistle. The restless stars looked like torches in the indigo sky, and the land below so small that he fancied he could see the Sierra Blanca like a mere hill of guano far below, and the Jornada del Muertos beyond it, and the curve of the earth, and the edge of the sun hiding behind it.

By and by Hull's horse came up the trail, chewing the end of the branch to which its reins had been knotted. Hull climbed up. Slattery eyed him sourly for a moment, but, being no fool, got up to beg a ride. "Stranger, you saved me, and I ain't ungrateful, but—"

Hull shook his head. "I swore an oath to see justice done."

Slattery noticed for the first time that they were not alone. A line of Apache braves sat astride horses all along the ridge. He saw their black livery and recognized his own horse with a Mescalero elder sitting in the saddle. Many guns trained on him, but the last thing they wanted to do, just now, was shoot him.

"Who the hell did you swear to?" Slattery screamed.

Hull nodded at the Indians. "To them," he said, and rode away.

Shadow Empire

March 13, 1900
Fort Sill, Oklahoma

Gray dust clouds rose up like weary ghosts off the flat, fallow fields around the Comanche reservation. Doors swung in the wind and slammed into the clapboard walls of the shacks as the cavalry troopers rode through. Except for a three-legged dog hell-bent on eating itself, they saw no sign of life.

"I sorely wish I knew where they went, Major," said Oliver Stickney, the Indian station agent. "It's not like there's anywhere for them to go anymore."

Major Cawthorne looked fit to break Stickney's reedy neck, but he turned his fury instead on the silent rider who stopped his painted horse and dismounted beside the slanting shacks that whistled like tuneless flutes in the wind.

"These are your people, Hull!" snarled Cawthorne. "If they've gone off the reservation again, it won't be the old war-path! They'll be tracked and put down like dogs!"

Inigo Hull stood motionless with his eyes roving the horizon in the failing purple-gray light. His long braided hair, the color of steel dust, brushed back by the wind, revealed the gruesome scars where other men had ears. One weathered, steady hand rested upon the hilt of one of the twin coffin-handled Bowie knives in his belt. The other hung perilously close to his sidearm, a .36-caliber, twelve-shot Navy revolver. His finely wrinkled copper face and deep green eyes were unreadable. The words from his unmoving lips galvanized Cawthorne like gunpowder in the Major's brain.

"If you'd have my help finding them, Major, you'll treat them just like human beings. But never call them *my* people."

Cawthorne spurred his horse to ride up on Hull, but seemed to choose his next words very carefully. "You've been paid well enough to ignore my bad manners, Hull. Mr. Stickney has a peapod for a pecker"—the Major acknowledged the Indian station agent with the slightest of nods—"but he's right. There's no frontier to light out for anymore, so they're bound to go raiding again. And hell itself will be shamed by my vengeance, if those goddamned savages spill a single drop of white blood on my watch."

Hull turned and regarded Cawthorne with a crooked smile. If the Kotsotekas of old had gone on the warpath again, they wouldn't need Hull to find them. The smoke from their raiding would block out the sun from here to Matamoros. If they had horses and weapons and hope; if they were not two hundred sick old men and women and hungry children who had never known the open plains, then nothing but the whole Union army would stop them. But nothing remained of the proud Comanche band that once ruled the southern plains, only stories in books and this open grave of a reservation.

Stickney slipped from his stirrups and hurried over to Hull as the irate Major snapped orders at his men. "Please don't take it hard, Mr. Hull. The major doesn't understand them—"

"And you do?"

Stickney flushed and puffed up. "Sir, I love them as I would my own children! The government gives me less every year, but I try to do right by them. They have schools and churches, and land to farm, if they'd only apply themselves to it. I've done everything I could to make this a home . . ."

Hull turned away to look in the unglassed window of the

nearest shack. Tin plates and the remains of a day-old hardtack and mush supper sat on the table. In a corner, a bow and a bunch of long, slender arrows leaned against a cracked and faded portrait of Jesus. Piles of discarded clothing—ugly un-dyed homespun cotton and wool agency garments—lay on the floor, like shed cocoons.

Oklahoma, a Choctaw name, meaning "red people." For the hundreds of thousands of years the Indian had lived in Ameri-ca, only this dry, sour land between Kansas and Texas had gone unclaimed. The Wichita and Pawnee who passed through these parts had all but forgotten the old legends, but they instinctive-ly avoided it. So naturally, for over fifty years, the white man had tried to dump every Indian here and forget them.

But even the Great White Father's worst promises could only be kept for so long. Less than a hundred miles away, the Oklahoma settlers, with their fat, unprotected ranches and huge stock herds, pressed ever closer into Indian Territory.

Hull fixed his unblinking eyes on the Indian agent. "A man came from outside and preached, told them stories, taught them new songs." It was not a question.

Stickney went pale and nodded. "I didn't think any harm could come of it, but he—"

"They went away to dance on a hill last night, and when the morning came they were gone."

"You know this man? Has this happened before?"

Watching the cavalry troopers ransack the shacks, Hull nodded. "Every time they've ridden off the reservation, it was because the land was too small, too sour, to live on, and every time they have been punished with worse land, and less of it. And this summer—"

"Yes," Stickney admitted, "there's to be a land lottery. They won't farm it, so someone else will. They won't grow up. I tell you, if only I could make them see. I admire them and I don't care who knows it, but they're like damned children! And now they've run off again."

"No. They have gone home."

Hull turned to look on as Major Cawthorne rode over to speak with a gaunt, graying man in a fringed buckskin coat and a long, deep groove of a scar splitting his sallow face from chin to widow's peak. The older man tipped his slouch hat to Hull as he heard the Major out.

"There is no home for them on the Llano Estacado anymore," Stickney said, "and nothing but fences in every direction. I tried to make them see—"

"Show me the hill," Hull said.

"We tried tracking them, Mr. Hull. There's no sign of them after they gathered on White Widow Hill."

Hull climbed onto his horse and reined it around to face the open plains, where a single perfect dome of a hill rose above the cottonwood trees two miles to the west.

"That's because they never came down."

Thunderheads rolled down from the north to snuff out the yellow gibbous moon. Searching by lantern light, it took less than an hour to find the hastily buried door into White Widow Mound.

Major Cawthorne had mustered thirty riders and twenty pack mules carrying ordnance, rations, and a Hotchkiss revolving cannon on the shoulder of the steep, strangely barren mound. He sat upon his horse and snapped orders at his men, but there was little to do until the scouts returned from inside the mound.

A driving rain soaked them and turned the baked red soil to streaming mud. Arguments cropped up among the troopers over whether the squirming black toads everywhere underfoot had wriggled up out of the earth or fallen with the downpour.

Hull and Stickney stood away from the others, on the flat summit of the mound, watching the circling patterns of dancing footprints dissolve into mud.

A low, shapeless green-black boulder squatted in the center of the abandoned dancing circle. Eroded down to a humble stub by eons of weather and worshipful hands, the stone bore no sign of its original form or purpose, but Hull stood staring at it in the pelting rain and the guttering light as if he saw much more than a stone, until Cawthorne's scouts returned, an hour later.

"Those clever devils," Cawthorne crowed. Grudging respect for his wily foes made his voice sound almost romantic. "There's no end to their cunning, is there, Roherty?"

The scarred man in the buckskin coat gobbed a lunger down the shaft. "Any slicker, and they'd have a bushwhacker gunning for us from behind, or better yet, right in our midst." Tobin Roherty tipped his hat again to Inigo Hull. "So this hill's got holes in it. But they ain't gophers. More than likely, it comes out in a canyon or another such anthill, somewhere in a day's ride. Have your scouts fan out and run them down."

"Mr. Hull doesn't seem to think so," Cawthorne snapped. "And my scouts couldn't find any passage but the one that goes down."

"This is a remarkable discovery," Stickney babbled. "I studied anthropology in Chicago and wrote my dissertation on the Hopewell Mound culture. I postulated contact with southwestern and Aztec cultures, but I never dreamed their empire stretched so far . . ."

Hull said, "You have no idea how far this empire stretched, or how deep. You think this land is new and easily won, but it is older than anything you can imagine, and your people have not yet begun to pay for it."

Stickney shivered and turned away from Hull, which was just as well. The half-breed had lived with bigotry all his life, but found he had still less patience for those who put the red man on a pedestal.

Hull had led men he trusted into this darkness before, and always returned alone. If he had to go one last time, he could not ask for better company.

Hull knew Major Randolph Cawthorne by reputation. Ten years ago in the 7th Cavalry, Cawthorne won a Medal of Honor for his service at Wounded Knee. He must believe history was repeating itself just to make him a colonel.

Tobin Roherty, the last of the old Texas scalp-hunters, ran down and harvested more than eight hundred arguably Apache trophies before no less a hand than Geronimo's had split his face with an axe. They'd both chased the same bounties more than a few times, and Hull had found him to be somewhat less of a blood-simple butcher than legend had it, and maybe even a better shootist. He tracked the infamous Green Gang to their nest in Locustville, but burned them out rather than bring them back for the bounty, when he learned what they really were . . . but that was a long time ago. Last Hull heard, Roherty was touring Europe with a circus, yet here he was. He probably thought this job would be even easier.

The Pawnee scouts reported that the tunnel turned in a tight spiral within the mound and continued downwards on a steep, paved slope, with no branching tunnels. They had turned back when the tunnel abruptly opened on a cavern too large for their torchlight to reach the far wall.

Cawthorne ordered his men to dismount and lead their horses. The first horse balked, then reared and kicked a handler's teeth in, when he tried to drag it into the mound. "Smart horse, put him in charge," someone said. Uneasy laughter ran down the column.

"Congratulations, ladies," Cawthorne shouted. "You've all been busted down to infantry!"

Grumbling men stripped the gear off their horses and formed a marching column.

"We will go down this road on foot to wherever it leads," Cawthorne barked, "and we will bring the marauding Comanche to heel. We will not be cowed by tall tales or Ghost Dance horseshit from the diligent pursuit of our duty. We will return the fugitives to their homes, or we will leave their scalps at the gates of Hell."

The troopers raised a querulous cheer and began to file into the narrow tunnel. The mules brayed and bit each other, but followed the men out of the rain and into the deeper dark.

Stickney carried a carpetbag and a canteen, but no weapons. "Someone must plead the case of sanity. And if Cawthorne won't listen, at least he'll restrain himself, with witnesses present."

"You should stay," Hull said. "Someone will have to stay behind to watch for the preacher when he comes back for more."

Stickney shrugged. "Nobody here needs me."

Hull led his horse down from the peak and handed its reins to a cavalry sergeant. A pouch of jerky, a stick of chalk, and a bandolier of rifle bullets were all he took from his saddlebags.

His hand went to a blue-gray coin on a rawhide thong around his neck. As Stickney watched it in the moonlight, the star-shaped coin twisted and twirled, and strained toward the open tunnel.

"After you, Mr. Hull," Tobin Roherty snarled, cutting a deep bow at the mouth of the tunnel. "I'll just bet you know the way."

October 20, 1890
Mt. Shasta, California

In the last flare of failing sunlight, the snow-capped flanks of the Trinity Mountains were transformed into a vast black beast, shaggy with pine forests and bristling with claws and fangs of jagged lava rock. Worlds away from the played-out goldfields, the fenced-off ranches and respectable boomtowns downstate, the country here was still so wild, it was the only place where the Union Army was forced to admit it lost a war to redskins. This was no place to live or get rich, but there was no end of places to hide.

"You sure this is the right place?" Captain Boyer shouted back up the pass at the grizzled, silver-haired scout as their posse picked its way down the loose scree and jutting boulders that choked the winding trail into the nameless alpine valley.

Hull surveyed the mountains rearing up all around them like waves on an angry ocean, and spat tobacco juice at the moon. "This is where it was," he replied.

"Well, damn my over-civilized eyes," Boyer said. He took up his field glasses and lensed the tapering valley below. "I see nothing but dirt." He said it wonderingly, as if nobody had told him it would be so.

"See there," Hull pointed down at the broad, featureless field of raw, red-brown earth, three acres across and eight deep. "That low place there was the main drag. And that stub of a post with a rag at the top . . . that's a flagpole. It was on the roof of the hotel."

Captain Boyer lowered his glasses and turned to study Hull the way they all did, the first time they thought he was pulling their leg. Hull made a stone mask of his face and hoped Boyer had heard the stories about the cavalry officers who had chosen not to believe Inigo Hull.

When the rest of his platoon had caught up and the pack wrangler had cursed the last of his mules up over the pass, Boyer rode recklessly down the shifting defile and into the empty valley. Hull followed close behind, reining his painted mare back when her hooves sank into the soft, freshly turned earth.

Unlike everything else in this part of the country, the town of Tolerance was not founded by the victors or victims of the goldfields. No one knew who claimed the land or built the perfect little mountain town, but the whispered word had gone out to every corner of the West that there was a place where everyone was welcome, and any man or woman who could work would be given a stake. The luckless losers, the mudsills and misfits, children of slaves, the Mex peasants and the Indians fled the dying silver towns and feudal ranches and fenced-in reservations to come and start over.

Never did the name appear in any newspaper or advertising circular, and no map showed the town; but the rumors and gossip set thousands to searching, until the word began to turn sour as most gave up or were never heard from again. Only last winter did Hull learn from an old fellow cavalry scout that there was such a place, and where it was hidden.

Hull was hot to get there, but he got waylaid by other work. He was still half-starved and badly frostbitten from hunting the Wendigo of Wind River a week before, but he rode out of Wyoming after a vivid dream of the earth eating a house filled with children. His worst suspicions had been justified, but he feared that this trap had only been sprung by his approach.

Captain Boyer dismounted and stood at the foot of the half-buried flagpole. He took his hat off, but not to salute the mud-caked rag of Old Glory. He fanned his pale face and swore as Hull dropped from his saddle to join him.

"Stage driver said the town was gone," Boyer said, "but I never took it to mean . . . literally *gone* . . ."

"The mountains hereabouts are hollow," Hull said, "rotten with lava tubes. The town was buried, but the people have been taken below."

"Surely we won't find survivors down there—"

"If we move fast, we can pick up their trail."

"This wasn't an Indian raid, Mr. Hull. The Modocs are long gone. It was a landslide. There could be survivors in the hills. Watkins," he called to his sergeant, "detail three search parties—"

Hull spat discreetly and muttered in the captain's ear, "You send them out, they'll never come back." Boyer turned a withering stare on him, but Hull had felt worse. "Look around you, Captain." Hull tried to keep the steel from his voice, but his patience was wearing thin, and he couldn't begin to explain what they were facing. "Look at the peaks and the hills above us. There've been no snows and no quakes here, this season. This town was *buried*."

Boyer wisely held his tongue, turning to set a detail digging around the flagpole.

They had only just plunged their shovels into the soft soil when they heard the tolling of the bell.

The leaden clangor rolled down the desolate valley like a death-knell for the five hundred and eighteen souls of Tolerance, California, but steadily rose from the measured tones of mourning into an unhinged jangling, to a sustained shriek of metallic insanity.

With Boyer and his men still casting about for the source, Hull leapt into the saddle and rode up the far slope to a spur of rusty red lava rock overlooking the sad, empty valley.

Perched atop the outcropping was a humble whitewashed chapel with a crooked steeple. The woods crowded up close behind it in a dense, black picket line. Higher and louder the bell rang and rang.

Hull slipped his Sharps buffalo rifle out of its scabbard as he leapt from his horse behind a sturdy pine. He felt no one watching him, but he itched all over with the sense that he was going into this like a hand into a glove.

Captain Boyer rode up and ordered his men to secure the chapel. The young officer's excitement was like a wet cat in his pants. A self-described Indian expert, he'd eaten up all the dime novels and fabulist lies packaged as histories at West Point, and no doubt relished the chance to test his mettle against them.

The narrow windows of the chapel were boarded up from within, and the doors, though battered and separated from their hinges, stood up to his shoulder. Pews and broken lumber were stacked against them, but Boyer's men easily forced them open.

The bell fell silent.

They blundered into the chapel expecting to find no one alive, but they found no one and nothing at all. A sinkhole twenty feet across gaped in the rough-hewn knotty pine floor, which had given way beneath the besieged parishioners' feet.

Hull crossed the empty chapel with his rifle in one hand and his pistol drawn in the other. He approached the pit and looked down, seeing only splintered debris on the floor of a plunging lava tube. Warily circling the pit, he peered up into the steeple. A flutter of gingham skirt caught his eye, and then the barrel of a shotgun winked and blasted at him.

Hull rolled behind a pew. Three troopers returned fire into the steeple. Their bullets rang the bell and sent a slim girl's body tumbling out of the steeple to crash on the pulpit.

Boyer charged into his men's sights and almost got himself cut in two. "Cease fire, damn it!"

Hull approached the girl. She was scarcely older than thirteen, and quite pretty by white men's standards, before she was scalped. Her naked skull wept in sympathy with the delta of blood pooling around her midriff, where her hand clutched a grievous belly wound like a bouquet of wet red roses.

"Why the hell did you shoot at us, girl?" Boyer demanded. His eyes were as wet and red as her belly.

"He . . . He s-s-said . . ." her breath hitched and rattled in her chest, but she struggled to sit up and reach out. Boyer sought to steady her, but she pushed him aside to point at Hull. "He said . . . you'd come . . . too late . . ."

"Easy, girl," Boyer murmured, lifting her head to drink from his canteen. Hull moved to stop him, but it hardly mattered. She was bleeding to death. "Where's everyone gone? What happened to your people?"

"End times coming . . . judgment trump sounded deep in the ground. Preacher called us to church . . . town got swallowed up . . . Devils come up out of the earth and beat on the doors, but he said we'd be safe so long as we followed him. He took us down where we'd be safe, but . . . yonder hole goes straight down to Hell . . . He took me aside and . . ." She brushed the sticky dome of bone where her hair had been and drifted off until Boyer shook her. "Preacher, he said to wait on that one . . ." Her bloody finger pointed at Hull.

Hull asked, "What did he say?"

"Father Malachai, he said . . ." Her eyes were cloudy glass beads, her breath cold puffs of mist, as if she lived only to deliver this message. "He said . . . if you hurry . . . he might let you catch him."

Relief flooded her face as she died.

"There's no way in hell we're going down there," Boyer gasped. His eyes were wide, but saw nothing. The darkness and enclosed space of the lava tube had already stolen his nerve.

"We have no choice," Hull answered. "Your men outside are all dead."

"The hell you say—" Boyer and his men ran for the door, but Hull seized his arm. "How do you know all this, damn you, if you're not a part of it?"

Sergeant Watkins charged outside, fired once, then screamed. A pattering like hailstones pelted the walls and roof of the chapel.

"They'll kill you just as quick," Hull said, "if you try to run. If they offer to spare your life, don't take them up on it."

The other two troopers fired out the cracks in the windows. "There's nothing out there! What do we do?"

Boyer clutched at Hull's arm. "What's out there, damn it? What are they?"

"Once they were men like yourself, who had all that men could wish for. Now, they are much more than men, and much less than human."

Hull tossed a rope down into the pit and tied it to the pulpit. "You can take your chances outside, or follow me. But choose quickly . . . the church is on fire."

March 14, 1900
White Widow Mound, Oklahoma

They marched through coiling tunnels like the spiral of an infinite snail shell. They followed fresh footprints in soft green sand through a vast cathedral of a cavern hung with glittering crystal chandeliers, and descended a tapering chimney with treacherous switchbacks carved into its metamorphic walls.

As the hours dragged out and the tangible darkness and pregnant silence began to take its toll, the troopers left off with their raucous songs and idle talk, for the cascades of distorting echoes made them uneasy and surely announced their position.

They emerged in a massive natural amphitheatre lit by huge, bumbling fireflies. Refilling their canteens at a brook meandering among colossal stalagmite towers, they caught fist-fuls of blind albino crayfish, and then repented of it when they turned vicious, and compared maps and compass readings. Needles spun wildly, then fixated on some random point, only to drift and spin without rhyme or reason. Cawthorne declared that they'd marched seventeen miles, though how deep they were, no one could hazard a guess.

Hull and the three Pawnee scouts spread out to find the walls and any exits. Hull returned first, having chalked a descending passage bearing recent smoke-stains, but Stickney spotted him consulting his weird coin.

Another scout shouted for the major. He led them to a blind niche in the cavern wall. Tucked away inside it was the ravaged corpse of an old Comanche woman. She lay naked and gutted from neck to pelvis, with her entrails carefully laid out upon her hands. A black circle drawn around the body seemed to hold at bay the bloated black toads that sprawled around its border as if worshipping the murdered woman.

"Savages don't take long to turn on each other, do they?" brayed Tobin Roherty.

"This was no cold-blooded murder," Stickney piped up. "The forced march probably killed her. Notice how little blood was spilled. This all happened after she died. If I'm not mistaken, it's a form of divination, isn't it, Mr. Hull? Haruspices in ancient Rome would read animal entrails to discern the will of

the gods, and Aztecs would do the same with human prison-
ers——"

Cawthorne lifted the heart out of the dead woman's hand
and threw it into the stream. "I've had quite enough of your
history lectures, Mr. Stickney. It matters not a whit what they
hope to gain by this barbarity. It only matters that they're slow-
ing down." Cawthorne wiped his bloody hand on the Indian
agent's cheek. "It's still warm, isn't it?"

Stickney shook with rage. "Major, if they're so committed to
this pilgrimage, how do you propose to peaceably bring back
two hundred Indians with only thirty men?"

Cawthorne didn't deign to answer, but Tobin Roherty cack-
led and replied, "I reckon we brought more than two hundred
bullets."

The other two scouts returned then, with one hanging on
the other's arm. His face was swollen and drooping with his left
eye closed over. His left arm hung limp at his side. "Spiders bit
him," said his mate. Cawthorne refused to let the Pawnee ride
one of the mules, but let him have a few good pulls of whiskey
before they set out.

Mopping his face with a handkerchief, Stickney jogged to
catch up to Inigo Hull, who walked on ahead to stay out of the
troopers' torchlight.

"I heard the agent I replaced tell stories about the Ghost
Dance, and I couldn't help but wonder about this ritual they
did on the mound. This was some new kind of Ghost Dance
that happened here, wasn't it?"

"Not like the Ghost Dance at all. If their hearts are set upon
the Backward Path and they are willing to pay its price, then
this dance will work."

"But it's madness! Surely they can't really believe magic will
save them——"

"Nothing else has worked. Is Walking Tree still the chief of the Kotsotekas?"

"He died just this past winter, I'm sorry to say. Pneumonia."

Hull took off his hat. "Walking Tree was always a coward. But he might have stopped this. The man who led them away, did you see him?"

"I did, briefly . . ."

"What do you remember about him?"

The question threw Stickney into a long pause. He hesitated, as if trying to recall a long-ago dream. "I was quite taken in by him. A grandfatherly fellow, but you know, it's odd, I can't quite recall what he looked like . . . Well-spoken, charming. He was hardly a firebrand like Wovoka or Tenskwatawa. He was a half-Cherokee Baptist minister, according to his papers. Wanted to preach the gospel to the Kotsotekas, so I let him.

"Of course, when they left their homes in the dead of night to carry on under the full moon, I was afraid . . . for them, of course. Every attempt to revive the old ways only stirs up trouble."

"Did you hear the songs? What was the name they chanted when the chanting turned to screams?"

"How did you know—?" Stickney started, but the effort of keeping pace with Hull's long, driven stride forced him to save the breath. Halting, he blurted out, "*Sadogwa,* or something like it. That's what they were calling out, over that hideous stone on the mound. *Sadogwa.*"

Hull whirled on him with such heat that Stickney flinched. "Sounds carry down here," the half-breed hissed. "And something is always listening."

They scurried through narrow fissures like bubbles blown in the living rock and marched on broad, buckled causeways like misplaced fragments of the Appian Way. Cawthorne ordered brief rests whenever the terrain allowed, but none of the men seemed willing or able to relax. Though gripped by an oppressive, moody silence, they seemed to have lost the rhythms of sleep and exhaustion and shuffled ever deeper into the earth with the fatalistic dread of men lost in dreams.

For nowhere but in dreams could there be any place like this. They descended a spiraling trail that wound around an inverted castle of onion-dome stalactites and fluted minarets that hung from the roof of a seemingly bottomless pit. They slogged over a desert of quartz spires with jagged facets that sliced their boots. The men wrapped bandanas over their mouths to filter out the razor-edged dust stirred up by their passage.

Where the crystalline floor became as clear as ice, they tried not to look at the squirming, blinking things trapped within it. Four of the mules dropped dead in their tracks, vomiting blood in the crimson hoofprints of the pack train. Nobody complained or demanded that they return to the surface. Nobody spoke at all, if they could help it.

Presently they emerged into a cavern so vast that its far walls were lost in a lurid blue glow, and Cawthorne ordered the lamps and torches doused. Some of the men gave a numb cheer, for they believed they had escaped from the caves and found the surface.

"Damn you lop-eared nimrods," Roherty jeered, "if that's the moon, you can call me Crazy Horse."

The gloom was saturated rather than dispelled by a coldly glowing cobalt sphere some miles in diameter, hanging in a vault of glowering stone clouds. Great screeching flocks of birdlike things swept by overhead—misshapen cousins to bats, eyeless, white and bigger than pelicans.

The floor of the cavern dropped away in sweeping terraces

to a boundless plain of shifting blue shadows. Sparks and green gas-jets fired in the murky distance, suggesting the impossible silhouette of a city.

By Cawthorne's count, they had marched for thirty miles. The dazed troopers stumbled over the summit and took the switchback trail down the mountain. In the lead, Hull froze and motioned for the column to seek cover. Roherty and Cawthorne joined him where he knelt behind a boulder.

"We are not alone," Hull said.

Roherty drew his celebrated silver Colt Enforcers and brashly leapt out from cover. "It's about time you cowards showed your faces—holy shit!"

"I can't see anything!" Cawthorne shouted. "Where are they?"

"Everywhere," Hull said. As their eyes adjusted to the indigo gloom, the others saw he was right.

The terraced mountainside was crowded with human forms—hundreds of men and women bent over irrigated paddies to tend a bumper crop of deformed, fleshy vegetables studded with jewel-like, idiot eyes.

The freakish fruits of their harvest were gathered in huge lead carts, which descended the mountains on tracks like cable cars. The laborers were naked but for the filth of their work, pale skins almost translucent in the unwholesome blue twilight. Most were ravaged by terrible, unhealed wounds, and many were missing limbs; but their clever masters had grafted shears, shovels, rakes, and cleavers to the stumps. One and all, they wore rawhide leather masks, tied taut over their faces with no holes for eyes or mouth.

Tobin Roherty stood surrounded by them, yet unmolested, unnoticed. Wonderingly he cuffed a blind, silent worker with one of his guns, and chuckled when it went on with its mute labor. "You all see something fishy in this picture?"

"They wouldn't believe me!" Cawthorne drew his saber and stalked along the ranks of oblivious slaves. "Nobody would listen when I tried to show them what these red devils are capable of! These are *white men!*"

Stickney approached Hull. "They're in some sort of mesmeric trance. I've heard tales of such cases from Haiti."

"There's no saving them," Hull replied. "The Empire of K'n-yan was built upon the labor of the dead."

"Rest easy, son," Cawthorne said to a kneeling male slave, "we've come to save you." Slashing the leather straps holding the mask on the slave's head, the major parted the mask and ripped it away.

The slave's head tilted back as if to gasp for air and take in the dim blue light, but he could do neither.

His mouth and nostrils were stitched shut with sinew thread. His eyes had been scooped out, and the sockets stuffed with quartz crystals that reflected in the blue light in a glittering mockery of life. Tufts of blond hair wafted away from the slave's rotting scalp like molted feathers.

Cawthorne went limp with shock. The unseeing slave returned to work. His saber shook at his side as he looked over the armies of hooded slaves on all the terraces below. "Remember this abomination, boys, when you have those savages in your sights. This is what they'll do to you and yours!"

Suddenly he whipped around and hacked with his saber. The slave's severed head tumbled into the foamy black water, while the headless corpse went on reaping.

"Sergeant Jarvis! Assemble the Hotchkiss gun."

Hull tried to stop him. "We should press on. The *y'm-bhi* will harm no one if we leave them to their work."

"*Their work!* They've taken white slaves! They've butchered and bewitched them and made a mockery of death!" Cawthorne drove Hull to the edge of the path with his saber thrust out, as if he meant to run the bounty hunter through. "Damn your half-savage blood if the sight of this atrocity doesn't make it boil!"

Hull took hold of the officer and shoved him back until he almost tripped over the headless slave. "The Comanche did not do this, Major. We are not in America anymore. We have wandered into the capital of an empire older than Christ, and greater than Britain or Rome. Its territories reached under the seas and down to the fiery heart of the earth. It fell into ruin eons ago, but this city lives still, for death is but one of its conquered kingdoms."

All had fallen silent to hear Inigo Hull, though he lowered his booming voice in sudden respect for the toiling dead all around them. "This is Tsath, the capital of the Shadow Empire of K'n-yan. And we are alive only so long as we amuse them."

Cawthorne looked around, but saw only the frightened faces of the living, surrounded by the faceless dead. "Where's my cannon, Sergeant?"

"She's dancin' if you're askin', sir," Jarvis called from the end of the train. The five-barreled machine gun rested on its wheels at the top of the mountain. Jarvis and one of the Pawnee scouts stood at the ready.

Even Major Cawthorne seemed to reconsider his rash order, when Sergeant Jarvis cried out, "You red bastard, you've stabbed me!"

Jarvis grappled with the spider-bit Pawnee scout, who drove a bayonet into the sergeant's belly as he roared an incoherent oath—"*Iä, Sadogwa! N'ggah kthn y'hulhu!*" The cysts in his eyes and throat burst and overflowed with tiny newborn spiders.

Jarvis shrieked and clawed the venomous swarm out of his face. The scout took the grips of the Hotchkiss revolving cannon. His eyes were weeping holes, but he scarcely needed to see the pack train and the idling cavalry troopers to rake them point-blank with five spinning barrels of piston-driven lead.

Four men and eight mules burst like wine kegs, while the surviving pack train bolted down the mountain. The troopers threw themselves behind the only available cover, among the rows of hooded slaves.

At such close range, the heavy shells chopped down the y'm-bhi like so much standing deadwood. Five more troopers were slaughtered before the posse rallied and cut down the infested scout. It took two of them to pry his dead, venom-swollen hands off the grips of the empty Hotchkiss gun.

Cawthorne swiftly took charge, ordering men to dress out the dead mules for meat and divide up the contents of their panniers, then detailed three men to take the Hotchkiss gun, though the last ammunition belts had run away with the pack train.

Stickney had cowered behind a dead mule through the shooting. Now he climbed over corpses to tug Cawthorne's sleeve. "Major, please, send the scouts back to the surface for reinforcements if you want to fight a war, but our orders are to find the Comanche."

Cold as an undertaker reading a bill, Cawthorne said, "Take your hand off me and get the hell out of my sight, or I'll have you shot."

"Look yonder, rubes!" Tobin Roherty pointed over their shoulders at the undead armies on the terrace. "I think we finally woke these boys up, Major."

The y'm-bhi hordes had silently regrouped and suddenly took hold of three troopers and summarily tore them apart. Relentless talons of naked bone shredded wailing soldiers and trampled their remains to get at the panicked survivors.

Surrounded by walls of groping hands, the company turned their backs to each other and fired into the shambling slaves, but their bullets only punched bloodless holes in unfeeling flesh. The circle collapsed under the sheer weight of bodies piling on top of them. The switchback trail down the mountainside vanished under a black tide of silent, faceless killers.

Tobin Roherty leapt up onto the shoulders of the fumbling dead and hopped from one to the next, firing into the mob and howling a wild rebel yell.

Hull unsheathed his bowie knives and hacked a clearing out of the forest of dead flesh all around himself, then ran along the edge of the uppermost terrace, shoving *y'm-bhi* slaves off the edge or into the paddies. Oliver Stickney and a Pawnee scout followed him, leaping over the limbless grotesques Hull left flopping in his wake.

Hull beheaded a slave, gutted another, and crushed the skull of a third with the pommel of his other knife, shoving the broken bodies into the path of their fellows, sending them tumbling at his feet. Without pausing to press the advantage, Hull leapt into a harvester's cart and drew his Navy revolver.

"Hull, wait!" Stickney hollered. "For the love of mercy, wait—" He dove headfirst into the cart just as Hull shot the brake cable. The Pawnee scout leapt for the falling cart, but it dropped out from under him so quickly that the leaden edge caught his legs and sent him spinning head over heels into the shredding claws of the *y'm-bhi*.

The cart gained terrible speed as it roared down the mountainside, flying past terraces and smashing away the grasping slaves that blocked the track. Stickney was flattened against the wall of the cart, while Hull clung to the prow and braced himself to shoot crawling slaves off the tracks.

When the cart slammed into the track's terminus, Hull leapt clear and rolled to a safe distance in the blue sand. Stickney was flung out of the cart in a flurry of crushed vegetables and landed badly on his right arm.

They lay on a subtly glowing desert plain on the desolate outskirts of a metropolis of onyx and obsidian, of towers, domes and pyramids to dwarf any under the sun; yet also a necropolis, unruined but seemingly uninhabited, and lit by unblinking, cold blue fires.

"Where are we?" Stickney moaned. "Is this Hell?"

Hull grimly set the Indian agent's broken forearm before he thought to reply. By then, Stickney was just delirious enough to accept his answer.

"Yes. But it is also home."

May 3, 1868
Fort Fetterman, Wyoming

The rising sun shone like a golden eye of judgment on the Platte River plains, but until this morning the rain had beat down on the red ground around Fort Fetterman for nineteen days. It was weather only fit for redskins, but Colonel Hemphill had insisted on riding at the earliest break in the storm. His prize white mare sank into the sucking mud fifty yards out of the gates and nearly drowned the colonel.

Before they could dig the mare out, the dawn patrol had come galloping in with a lost girl they'd found on the trail.

"Now, you just take a good long look," Barney Farquhar said to the girl, "and you speak right up if you recognize any of these bad boys."

Smiling eagerly, Farquhar dangled the flyblown bunch of

severed redskin heads for the girl, twisting the knotted ropes of hair in his grubby fist so she could see each face up close as it swiveled past her glazed, empty eyes.

"Leave her be, Barney," the ruddy-faced sergeant said, shoving the bounty hunter out the door and waving away the rest of the rabble who'd come to eyeball the girl. "She ain't pickin' none of your rotten fruit today. All you vultures, make yourselves scarce!"

The girl was starved and bloodied and scared out of her mind, with brambles and thorns woven into her hair. She belonged with the last wagon train that left the fort for Oregon three weeks ago. She told the men who found her that their guide led them into the Rockies, and that "the mountains ate them up." She would say no more, but the wound carved into her palm—parallel zigzag lines like a lightning bolt curling on itself, or a serpent eating its tail—was a silent scream that haunted the half-breed scout who found her.

Corporal Hull slouched in the doorway of the fort's telegraph office and watched Sergeant Truscott try to coax the girl out of her trance with a peppermint stick. He had never seen anyone look so lost, but he knew more than most, how she probably felt. Once, not so long ago, he had also wandered into a fort with all his life torn away.

He was born and raised a Comanche of the Kotsotekas, the warlike rulers of the southern plains from Kansas to Mexico. His mother died giving birth to him and he never knew his father, but every man in the tribe was his father until he was thirteen.

When he returned from his first buffalo hunt, he found the camp hysterical with mourning. The chief had been killed and mutilated in his sleep, and the shaman lost in madness after an evil dream. The new chief, a callow brave named Walking Tree who feared and despised Hull, called him a curse sent by the devils under the earth. The Kotsotekas cast Hull out with a buckskin bag full of white papers he couldn't read and a bloody blue wool coat. No other tribe would accept him, so he set out east for Fort Cobb.

The papers he carried identified him as the only son of Cadmus Hull, a Union Cavalry lieutenant and notorious deserter and renegade. He earned his keep as an interpreter and horse-breaker. No man on the post was his father, yet they taught him much until he turned sixteen and enlisted him as a cavalry scout. Though they never quite trusted him, they gave him work and a path to manhood.

At the bleeding edge of the settled frontier, Fort Fetterman oversaw the split of the Oregon and California Trails, and skirmished almost daily with one or another of five hostile tribes. While the Civil War raged back east, the wagon trains had flowed out of Fetterman like lemmings off a cliff into the lawless wilderness. Native scouts outnumbered the rank-and-file infantry, and the Indians raided the wagons without fear. But with the end of the war, the Union had turned its undiluted wrath upon the southern Plains Indians and beat them into accepting a treaty that would relocate them all to the badlands between Kansas and Texas. In another year the railroad would join the east with California, and the wagon trails would become cornfields and stockyards, enclosed in fences from sea to shining sea.

Hull knew that your place in the world could be ripped out from under you in less than a breath out here. You could get right with it however it all panned out, or you could go mad looking for the hidden hand that kept tearing it apart.

Hull stepped outside and watched the traffic passing through the fort and the trading post. He stuck close to the office, because they'd be sent out soon to find the girl's people.

The fair weather had set many trains to hastily setting out, despite the saturated ground. Their wheels bogged down and flung cakes of blood-red mud skyward as they passed through the open stockade gate. Greenhorns and religious fanatics on the trains might still get themselves killed, even without the natives' help.

A stranger surprised him. One moment Hull was alone on the creaking boardwalk outside the office door, and the next, a hand fell on his shoulder.

Later, Hull couldn't say whether he'd heard him speak first or just felt his presence and turned around. And what he heard—or what he thought he'd heard—left him flummoxed.

The words in his ear were a strange chain of sounds that no human tongue ought to be able to string together. And yet he thought he understood them, for he heard, in his mind, "The Road Below is open, boy. Will you come home now?"

Corporal Hull guardedly looked at the man, searching for some familiar sign, but he'd never seen this man before, and he was not Comanche.

Rawboned and compact, with white hair cropped just above the collar of his fringed buckskin shirt and tucked under a black, broad-brimmed drover's hat, the stranger looked more than half white. At first he appeared not much older than Hull, with a broad brow and sharply chiseled cheekbones, but the wrinkles around his cobalt blue eyes were spiderwebs with centuries trapped in them. His teeth were long and yellow, and finely etched with geometric symbols.

When Hull locked eyes with the stranger, he shrank inside himself as the stranger grew, until Hull was like a swaddled baby on a cradleboard or a man buried up to his neck in the sand. The face of the stranger looking down on him was like the sun, beams radiating from his eyes seeming to shine right through his skull, and everything Hull was, everything he knew, was laid bare and stolen away.

Suddenly they were just two men standing together in a muddy fort. Hull's brain somersaulted in his skull. He reached out to a post and clung to it until his knees stopped shaking.

"What did you say to me?" Hull asked.

The stranger's smile turned sad, and he gave Hull a pitying shrug as he passed by, saying, "I mistook you for someone else. Good day, my son."

Hull stared after the stranger until he heard the sergeant shout and the chow bell ring an alarm.

Barging into the office, Hull nearly got run over by a bellowing Sergeant Truscott. "*Murder!* A girl's been murdered in our midst! Shut that damned gate!"

Beyond Truscott, Hull saw the girl from the wagon train splayed out across the desk. In the middle of the telegraph office, in less than a few minutes, someone had cut her open from neck to crotch and filled her hands with her heart and liver.

Only then did Hull notice the bright red handprint on his shoulder, where the stranger had touched him.

Hull ran out onto the quadrangle, searching the sea of faces. A crowd massed at the office door, and the men at the gates were cursing in rounds. A wagon drawn by two oxen with a Mormon elder at the reins was bogged down in the gateway, and a gang of soldiers and civilians had been pressed to push it out of the mud. Hull saw a flash of dancing buckskin fringe among the mob. He dropped to one knee to see the smiling stranger duck under the wagon and pass out through the open gates.

"Stop that man!" Hull ran through the gates with his pistol drawn. He heard a great splash just beyond the open gate. He thought of the sea of sucking mud outside, and smiled.

The mud trapped his boots and he slid to a stop just outside the fort. The next wagon was hundreds of yards down the washed-out road, and no man or beast was anywhere in sight, except the sinking hindquarters of the colonel's unfortunate horse.

A bottomless lake of red ooze stretched out to the right of the trail. Hull got up and trudged to its unstable shore, bent and plucked the black drover's hat off the surface. A few bubbles broke through the stubborn scum, but of the stranger he saw no other sign.

With the Indian relocation going full steam down south, a full company couldn't be spared to run down the vanished wagon train. Hull and two Delaware scouts—Barking Bird and Left-Handed Jim—rode west on the Oregon Trail ahead of an expected party led by Colonel Hemphill, as soon as his new horse arrived from back east.

They rode hard for a week, stopping at trading posts and wagon camps beside every swollen stream. Nobody had seen or heard of the missing train, but everyone had a tale of someone who had dropped off the face of the earth in these parts. The Indians and settlers blamed each other with a blind symmetry that hinted at some invisible third party in the middle, craftier and crueler than either of its neighbors.

The old, half-blind French mother of the trading post agent at Goshen Hole set to cursing in her native tongue when she squinted at the crude sketch Hull showed around. She told him that the white-haired, blue-eyed half-breed had called himself Honest John. He came through preaching the End of Days and led a flock of scared settlers and Cheyenne Indians up onto a hilltop to be lifted to Rapture. In the morning they were gone, every soul, including her mother, sisters and brothers. The trader told Hull she was crazy. Honest John the preacher was a local legend that, if true at all, had occurred around 1810.

Hull and the Delawares rode out of the grasslands and into

the dry steppes of the Laramie Mountains, past wind-carved castles eroded to reveal the trapped bones of petrified thunder lizards. The sun beat down so hard that if you stood still, your shadow would burn into the rocks.

Two days into the high country, they found the mark.

It was carved into a lightning-struck oak with its roots snarled around a boulder the size of a house. If Hull had not committed the crude symbol to memory, until he saw it with his eyes closed, he might have missed it, and the hidden trail it pointed out of the jumbled, jagged rocks.

The trail was cut with fresh wagon tracks and took them up a sandy creek bed in the shadow of Black Mountain, where the Oregon Trail first began to climb in earnest up the eastern face of the Rockies. None of the scouts knew of any overland pass hereabouts. There were countless places to get lost, stuck, or ambushed.

Hull and the Delawares doggedly picked their way up the steep trail, then followed it into a rocky downward draw that meandered for two miles before ending in a box canyon. The walls loomed outward as they climbed nearly a hundred feet with no exit, but Hull was sure they'd come to the right place. When he dismounted, he began to see the jagged symbols chiseled in the sandstone everywhere he looked. In the lee of a boulder above the trail, he found a broken boot heel in a young lady's size, and a shard of bloody rock that she or someone else must have used to cut the image in her palm.

But the trail ended here, and no wagon train. No blood or spent bullets, no signs of a struggle. Whatever she had seen had not ended here. Hull went to the wall and ran his hands over the weathered granite, probing every natural facet and carved symbol until his numb, bloodied fingers found a seam that somehow felt like the handle of a door.

When he tugged at it, the entire face of the wall swung like a bank vault door on hidden hinges that gave not a groan until it revealed a cylindrical shaft, thirty feet in diameter, boring down into the mountain.

Before they even debated whether or not to enter it, the three scouts stood before the open door without speaking or looking at each other. White men might have known fear of the unknown that only fired their curiosity and crazy, perverse courage. But they had all heard tales of what lay beneath the earth, and to the Indians it was more frightening than Hell. The white man believed that bad souls went below the ground when they died to be punished. The Comanche believed that men had come up out of the earth at the beginning. Hell is all the more frightening if one has escaped it once already.

At last, Hull spurred his buckskin stallion over the threshold. The tunnel's unpaved floor was smoother than any white man's road and sloped gently downward as it delved deeper into the mountain. The Delawares followed only after Hull taunted them, but his excitement masked a creeping dread that something below *wanted* them to come.

The tunnel led them down for almost another mile, before they reached a massive natural cavern. The torchlit walls seemed to crawl with ornately carved snakes and stranger legless things of the earth and sea, far more complex and obscene than the crude imitations outside. Hidden among the crazed bas-reliefs were the handholds of ladders, which Hull traced up to recessed cliff-houses, tucked under the dripping, vaulted ceiling. They were of the Anasazi type found all over the Southwest, but much older, and hewn out of the black basalt walls rather than built out of bricks.

Everywhere they walked, the floor was crusted with black-red blood.

Hull led the terrified scouts around the walls of the cavern and found a steeply descending passage. A chill wind that reeked of carrion blew away their hats and snuffed their torches.

Hull heard a wet crunching and felt a spray of hot wetness across his face. Jim screamed and galloped off into the dark.

Hull fought to calm his stallion. He backed up until he hit a wall, struck a match, and lit his torch. Barking Bird lurched after him, his mouth mutely flapping. Above his nose, a hole the size of a fist had been punched right through his skull, but somehow he sat astride his palomino until another silent sharpshooter cut him down.

Hull saw something waiting just outside of the glow of the torch. Shambling, silent shapes pulled Jim out of the saddle and abruptly silenced his terrified horse.

Hull drew his rifle out of its scabbard. His horse reared up and whirled, poised to run, but no direction offered safety.

Something whooshed out of the dark and smashed his horse's head in. Hull saw a fist-sized ball of dull blue-gray metal crush the stallion's skull like a soap bubble. Something like a cannon, but utterly silent. Hull rolled off the horse as it toppled, and lay prone behind its spasming corpse. He cocked his Winchester and fired at phantoms.

They were men, or had been once. Naked and armed with tarnished silver cleavers or razor-beaked shears bolted to the stumps of severed limbs, they stumbled blindly toward Hull as if eager for the blessing of lead.

He hammered them down as fast as he could aim, but he could not kill them, for they had no heads to shoot. Limbs blown away and ribcages cracked to disgorge black, unbeating hearts, yet they kept coming.

In his short life, Inigo Hull believed he had faced every form of fear. Before he was seventeen, Corporal Hull fought in the Red

River Wars against his own people, and he had tracked down the Texarkana Walking Snake only a year before, so he was no stranger to bad medicine. But in his experience the dead did not walk, and nothing stood up to a well-aimed Winchester rifle. What crept ever closer to him with fumbling axes and groping, ragged claws was not only an inescapable death, but the crumbling of the last pillars of certainty in Inigo Hull's world.

At last he saw a face in the advancing, headless horde, and a familiar one. The stranger smiled knowingly as he pushed to the front of the mob and mockingly bowed to Hull, as if in surrender. He laid down an ornately carved tube of dull blue-gray metal like a blunderbuss, but with no hammer or moving parts. "You came almost before I called you. It must be Fate."

Hull shot from the hip and blasted the teeth out of that smile just before the howling death-wind returned and snatched away his light.

Something slashed at his face and tore his hat off. Hull retreated as he emptied his rifle. The downward sloping passage offered the only escape, but the slope soon became a slippery chute, and Hull rolled and tumbled down a polished stone slide.

He lost his rifle when he fell away from the slide completely, clawing through empty space and crashing into a bed of canvas and wire hoops. Bruised and shaken, he crawled out of the wreckage and struck a match.

He had landed on a wrecked Conestoga wagon that rested upon a mountain of broken rigs that spread out beyond the reach of his fire. Stagecoaches, buckboards, and a pathetic scattering of burst luggage added variety to the landscape. Empty gingham dresses and long johns lay splayed out over the wreckage like shed snakeskins. He could see no floor beneath the mound of wagons, and had no idea how high they were piled. Hundreds, thousands of people had come over the frontier in search of a home, of fortune and a fresh start, and instead they came to this.

The match burned his fingers, but when he threw it out, the awful wind came again, roaring out of a deeper crevice in the far wall of the ghastly dumping ground. Though it reeked of death and decay, he sensed that the breeze came from something very much alive though it feasted on death, and he had the queasy hunch that it was not a wind at all, but *breath*.

Fear paralyzed his mind, but his body took over with hard-won and deadly reflexes. Drawing his Colt, Hull hunkered down and waited out the torrential death-wind, then made a fresh torch and began to leap from one junked wagon to the next in search of an exit. He thought he heard rushing water ahead when he felt a wind at his back.

His legs were kicked out from under him. He fell head first into a steamer trunk filled with blank tombstone samples. Thrashing in the dark, he caught an arm and tried to snap it at the elbow, only to have it dissolve into cold smoke in his grip and then wrap around his throat.

Powerful hands slammed him against the polished marble tombstone. "You are blind now. Wait, and it will all come clear. This is what your eyes were made for."

Hull was startled to see a glint of what he took to be metal, shining in the absolute dark. His eyes were adjusting, but what he saw was the subtle blue inner glow of the eyes of his enemy.

Hull threw out an arm and grabbed the stranger's face. His thumbs dug for the eyes, but the head twisted until his fingers got caught between gnashing teeth. He found the gap where he'd shot three back teeth out, peeled the bullet-split cheek back to the ear, and squeezed as he was bit, digging his nails into the raw holes in his enemy's jaw.

His enemy screamed and spat out Hull's hand. The blood-curdling cry was pure exultation. "Oh, thank you for that! Why would any man not want to feel such quickening bliss?"

Hull took back his hand and tried to unsheathe his bayonet. "I am a Union Army scout. When I do not return, they will come in such numbers—"

The stranger's baying laughter turned to sneering words in his mind. *They'll come for a redskin scout?* "And what will they find?"

He did not see, but keenly felt, the chopping blows to his throat, liver, and kidneys that dropped him to his knees. His left hand was crushed under a heel until he dropped his knife. Stunned and helpless, he lay prone on the tombstone slab. A foot shod in a moccasin of leather too fine to be anything but human pinned his head to the marble, while an iron grip snapped his other arm at the wrist.

"How old are you, boy?"

Hull fought to control his agony before he answered. The words were some time, coming to his lips. "Twenty years. If I could track you down, they'll come—"

"You think *you* found *me?* Don't you know how long I've been calling you?"

Before he could answer, a relentless hand dug into his mouth and pried his jaw helplessly wide open. "You are old enough to pay for what you take."

Hull tried to bite back his screams, but when his back molar was wrenched out of his lower jaw like a cork from a jug, he was too weak with delirious pain to bite the stranger's hand.

"You could stop this, boy."

When the prying fingers took the second tooth, he could only moan as the agony engulfed him like the sun. It was a little thing, to lose a tooth, but the exquisite twanging of his nerves with each wrenching twist was like a revelation of how deeply enslaved he was to his body, and how helpless to save it.

"This body, this life, this world, it is all a prison, and it is all a lie. Free yourself!"

He lost a third tooth. A thin, whistling shriek came from Hull's chest, quite without breath or will behind it. Hull had escaped his body altogether, with its hopeless demands that it all stop, in death, if not in revenge.

"Everything mortal will fail you, boy. And when you die, you will come to us . . . but there are many roads."

Pain was a rushing river, but Hull fought against it to fight the stranger even as he was thrown over the shoulders of a beast that carried him on four legs, but stank like a man.

"Tell them to come. Tell them all to come and find me."

Hull was thrown off a ledge and fell into a chill wind and shrieking darkness. Wrapping his arms around himself, he thought of that awful breath from the deeper abyss and prayed, but before he could choose a god to beg, he smashed into a churning, icy whirlpool. The water restored him to his senses almost too late to save himself, but when he kicked for the surface, his head struck stone and sent him spinning in the lightless current.

He was found floating down the Laramie and dragged to shore by some Arapaho boys, who left him to the vultures when they saw he wore a blue Union jacket.

A fortnight later, He led Colonel Hemphill's cavalry detachment back to the box canyon. The wall was solid stone, with no trace of any door or of the missing scouts.

March 15, 1900
Outskirts of Tsath

While Stickney recovered his wits and breath, Hull rounded up the surviving pack mules and looted their panniers. He kept a string of four and cut the rest loose.

Gunshots and howled oaths rolled down from high up on the mountainside, but they were muted, muffled by the palisades of undead slaves swarming over them. Hull wasted a few shots on the distant knots of grappling bodies with his buffalo rifle, but he saw no point in going up after them.

Stickney saw it differently. "We have to go back." He sat on the lead mule with a rifle across the improvised saddle and his arm in a sling. "Without Major Cawthorne and his men—"

Hull turned and led the mule train back to the causeway that led to the city. "Without them, we may reach our destination before it is too late."

"You'd leave them to die?"

Without looking back, Hull said, "I *brought* them here to die. I only hoped they'd make a better show of it."

They passed huge granaries and warehouses with gaping doors through which the *y'm-bhi* pushed wheeled carts laden with the deformed harvest, and hurried past the nauseous pall of decay wafting from them.

"All that labor wasted to grow tainted food," Stickney said, "but who eats it?"

"The people of Tsath have outgrown the need for earthly food. But maybe it tickles them to have slaves wasting themselves in endless work."

"If they can make the dead walk and fight, then why do they hide down here? They could easily overthrow the Union and take back the whole damned country."

"They surely could, if they cared to. They conquered the world and stole the secrets of the gods long ago, but life became an empty game, and now they care only for dreaming. Only a few still take on flesh and walk in the world, to find fresh food and slaves and new players for their games."

"What kind of games?"

"They create suffering and horror as other races have created art, for its own sake. But one among them plays his games
with the old gods of the bottomless gulf, whom even the mad
half-ghosts of K'n-yan dare not worship."

"So he's brought the Comanche down all this way to teach
them to worship this—" Stickney caught himself just short of
blurting out the hideous name.

"Only the lowest things that live bow to Tsathoggua," Hull
hissed. "The Comanche are a broken people, but they must still
walk the Backward Path to N'kai to be cleansed. They have
much yet to lose—their pride, their pain, and their humanity—
before they can become his children. Then it will be too late to
save them or anyone else."

Stickney shook his head with frustration and rifled out
more questions, but the half-breed did not deign to answer
them.

The road crossed over a flooded cataract on a bridge carved
with entwined serpents and spiders. The two men, on occasion,
looked down to see the river choked with squirming black
toads.

Beyond the bridge they passed through a district of colossal
factories. Most of these were abandoned and buried under centuries of rust, but in the others, monolithic machinery
throbbed and roared, and eerie cobalt-glowing furnaces radiat-
ed pulses of blinding ball lightning high into the domed sky.
Hull saw Stickney raise a hand to shade his eyes against them,
and saw the living bones of his hand and arm through his
transparent flesh.

Legions of older, badly decayed y'm-bhi slaves tended the
furnaces and the infernal engines powered by their unholy fire.
Many were mutilated amputees or little more than skeletons,

and others were headless, with silver antennae jutting out of their exposed spinal columns. When one tumbled into the titanic, gnashing gears, more pressed forward to take their places.

The insane flurry of mindless activity was just like the mountain farms, Hull reflected, for the factories and dynamos seemed to consume and replace each other in a great circle of waste, and the unbelievable city they served was seemingly empty.

They crossed desolate arcades lined with ebony idols of obscene human-beast hybrid gods, and mirror-lined plazas where hydra-headed spires to dwarf the size of Gizeh or the decadent majesty of Babylon strained up to fuse with the mist-shrouded roof of the great cavern. They detoured into empty amphitheatres and arenas where hapless *y'm-bhi* gladiators silently battled monstrous automata, and fled ghostly waves of bodiless applause. They hastened down twisted avenues lined with temples and sacred abattoirs clogged to their golden rafters with unclaimed sacrifices, but they never saw a single living soul.

It was the most magnificent city ever constructed by human hands, and yet its unrelieved blackness and maddening, abandoned density, and the eerie shimmer of dim cobalt light upon its relentless bas-relief façades, and the drifting indigo mist that seemed to follow them everywhere, made the eyes play tricks on their fevered brains. Stickney told Hull that the exotic otherness of Indian artifacts had always fired his sense of wonder at the infinite variety of human ingenuity, but that he hungered for some proof that these horribly debased, decadent monsters were no kin of humankind. Hull ignored this.

"You said the people of Tsath were dreamers," Stickney said much later, to break the stifling silence. "Are they sleeping, or are they dead? I just can't believe that such an advanced society would just die out . . . they are dead, aren't they?"

Hull was visibly unnerved by the city, but he answered in a tight, low voice. After all they'd seen, he now needed to talk. "At the height of their power, the shamans of K'n-yan mastered the secrets of matter and spirit. They used the dreaming engines of Yoth to make wealth and whatever else they desired, and even new bodies when their old ones died."

"This should have been a paradise," Stickney said. "Something must have poisoned their minds, as lead poisoned the Caesars of Rome."

Hull scoffed. "All men carry the seeds of their own ruin. Death—and life—lost all meaning. But immortality did not make them gods."

"But there were some who rejected this way of life, weren't there? The lost tribes, like the Moundbuilders and the Anasazi, must have come up from the underworld thousands of years ago. But they were never so advanced—"

Hull nodded. "They worked hard to forget. When the white man came, he found the people spread across the land, speaking many tongues and fighting among themselves. He found them easy to conquer because of their differences, yet everywhere he found the scattered children of the same, forgotten parent. Some came to America by sea, or across the ice from the east, but nearly every tribe recalls that their ancestors simply walked out of a hole in the earth on the day of creation.

"The Olmecs and Toltecs, the Mayans and Aztecs and the tribes of the Plains were the last to leave K'n-yan, when the great islands of Atlantis and Lemuria sank beneath the sea and the Seven Cities sealed itself away from the outer world.

"The ones who stayed behind soon grew bored with their paradise and hungered for oblivion. They began to worship the old gods in the black gulf of N'kai, and many took the Backward Path to assume the first forms, before the cult of

Tsathoggua was abolished."

"But there must have been hundreds of thousands," Stickney's words raced from his mouth, "in a city this size. What happened to them? Because there's nobody here."

Hull stopped the mule train and slipped his Sharps rifle into its scabbard on his back. "They are all around us."

Ahead of them, the luminous blue mist wound through the columns around a desecrated onyx altar before an empty pedestal. The mist billowed and filled the avenue, but when Hull forged ahead it recoiled and regrouped until it seemed to hide a solid, breathing form.

Something came lumbering out of the mists on all fours with a rider upon its elephantine back, but the grotesque beast was itself more than half human. Its thick legs ended in stout, spade-clawed digits with spurs of rudimentary thumbs. Its shaggy battering ram of a head sported a stout scimitar-shaped horn, but its broad, snarling face was that of a golden-haired man of saturnine features and a terrible, arrogant fury magnified by its brutish stupidity.

Stickney reined back his pack mule to retreat behind Hull. "Good God in heaven, what is it?"

"A *gyaa-yothn*," said Hull, with a grim smile. "Men remade as beasts of burden. And the masters of K'n-yan, in the flesh."

The rider controlled his mount with the whip of his mind and carried a weapon in each hand: in the left, a broadsword that whined like a buzzsaw with a revolving chain of steel teeth, and in the right, a blue-gray tube of otherworldly magnetic metal, like an elephant gun.

Regal of bearing and attired in robes of black leather and armored in silver and onyx jewelry, the rider bore only a distant kinship to the noble savages Stickney proclaimed to know and loved from his books. In the arrogant posture, the rich

clothing, and the bizarre weaponry, the man of K'n-yan reminded Hull of the alien images of Mayan emperors, mad with
their own false godhood and drunk on their own decay, and
the fanatical savagery of the Aztecs, in the forbidden manu-
scripts he'd studied to prepare for this day.

The retreating mist revealed, or created, a host of spectators among the columns all around them. Their jeweled black
robes and colorless, leprous faces evanesced in the false blue
moonlight. Their huge, cruel eyes sparkled with jaded lust and
unimaginable madness.

The rider spurred his man-beast to rear up on its hind legs,
and croaked a challenge. *"Kth-khkukak ssh'th ngluh X'n-yian!"*

Hull suppressed a chill at the guttural onslaught of alien
speech that only seemed louder when he stopped his ears, as if
the brittle words directly attacked his brain. But he stood his
ground and responded in kind. *"N'gluh ul M'l-akai xiu gk-vrsssh
N'kai."* The rider joined the host of spectral courtiers in rasping, indulgent laughter.

The snarling *gyaa-yothn* lowered its horny head to the
carved flagstones like a bull. The rider struck his humming
sword across his breastplate to make a fan of sparks, dug his
spurs into the man-monster's shaggy flanks, and charged.

Hull feigned ignorance of the attack until it was almost too
late, until he felt the man-beast's fetid breath on his face.

His eyes closed and head bowed, he pivoted to evade the
charge. His hands dropped to his belt, and the twin ten-inch
bowie knives slipped from their sheaths faster than thought.
One knife flashed out to parry a speeding spherical bullet from
the rider's silent rifle, while the other flew from his hand
straighter than a bullet, like the penetrating gaze of its wielder
congealed into steel.

The thrown knife struck the charging rider in his throat and half beheaded him. He flipped backwards off the man-beast's back, but his unmanned mount pivoted and charged again.

Hull unholstered his Navy revolver and shot point-blank at the monster's bony skull, but the bullets skated off it like rain off a hot skillet. The enraged *gyaa-yothn* hurled him aside to get at easier prey.

Too late to save itself, the lead mule bucked and turned under Stickney to meet the charge broadside. The terrified agent swung his shotgun at the onrushing beast and blasted its shoulder, to no effect.

The knurled horn of the *gyaa-yothn* plunged deep in the mule's ribcage. Tossing and bellowing in bewildered rage, the creature flung the impaled mule high over its head and dashed it to the flagstones, but couldn't dislodge it. Stickney was flung head over heels into space.

For all its powerful bulk and surprising speed, the *gyaa-yothn* was trapped. The gored mule, shrieking horribly and kicking out its last on the man-monster's horn, writhed and strained in its harness. The mule's teammates dug in their hooves and backed away, and a gruesome tug-of-war ensued.

Hull reloaded his revolver and rushed to disable the rampant man-beast, but three more warriors of K'n-yan materialized around him and, with yipping coyote cries of demented glee, dove on him with their whining knives.

Hull dodged two slashing saw-blades and stepped inside the arc of the third to slam his bowie knife into the mad attacker's ribs.

The broad blade skewered the warrior's heart, but Hull swung the twitching body into the path of his other enemies to deflect their stabbing swords. Through the kicking legs of his first victim, Hull shot the kneecap off another warrior, then blew his brains out as he toppled wailing to the ground.

His last attacker lunged at Hull's back and laid open his shoulder with a whining knife. Hull gasped as the blade's spinning chain bit deep into his flesh.

The wounded bounty hunter stumbled but spun on one knee to defend himself. The warrior jumped back and held the blood-streaked blade up to catch the blue false moonlight, howling to the starless sky as if he'd defeated Hull, and vanished in a tornado of cackling blue mist.

Hull freed his knife as the dead warrior disintegrated around it, and leapt onto the man-monster's back. The bucking beast tried to throw him off, but Inigo Hull had mastered wild horses before most children learn to walk. He straddled the bounding monster's broad back—shaped by centuries of breeding so no saddle was needed—just as it flung the dead mule off its horn and tried to roll over and crush him. Hull drove the massive blade up to the hilt in the monster's spine, just behind its armored skull, and jumped clear.

Every muscle in the mammoth body convulsed, until the creature almost seemed to recall its lost humanity and tried to stand on its hind legs. Only then, with a mournful whine like a half-remembered prayer, did it finally die.

Hull found Stickney lying face down on the flagstones with a curious retinue of elaborately scarred women of Tsath probing him with their needle-tipped fingers. They hissed and made the sign of Yig at Hull, then begged him to shoot them.

He found his other knife lying in the street with trailing wisps of electric blue mist clinging to it. The ghostly spectators bowed and murdered themselves with needles and knives and syringes filled with acid, and unraveled in scarves of icy blue mist, or just dissolved into the shadows, recharged by the sight of violence and inspired to commit some bold new atrocity. Long after they had faded away, their sneering, breathless laughter stirred the stifling air of the undead city.

The injured and unconscious Indian agent would only slow Hull down, but to leave him here would be crueler than to have left him with the soldiers. And in his own blinkered way, Stickney had tried to be kind to the people in his care. He might yet be of use.

He tossed Stickney's battered body over the next mule in the train and kicked it forward. He still felt eyes upon him, but the fickle, slithering focus of the city itself had already tired of him and turned elsewhere.

Presently he heard the gurgle of rushing water and turned down a wide staircase that ended at a pier overlooking a wide black river. Many of the pavilions and palaces above the river had collapsed into the oily current, and the looming idols at the head of each pier were corroded, faceless sphinxes. But still he felt something watching him.

A galley with a crew of twenty hooded *y'm-bhi* at the oars waited at the end of the pier. Hull dragged his mules onto the ship and cut the mooring lines.

The current was swift, and the galley had slipped out into the middle of the wide river before Hull smelled strange blood on the air and realized they weren't alone.

"Well hell," gloated Tobin Roherty. He held a cocked pistol to Stickney's head, and a riot gun aimed at Hull's heart. "Ain't you goddamned redskins jus' full of surprises."

June 24, 1876
Natchez, Mississippi

The next time he saw the stranger, Hull thought he was ready.

It was after they had tracked down the last cursed gold ingot from the Conquistador's cursed horde, and they were a week deep in celebrating. Hull had all but forgotten the stranger's face, which was just how the blue-eyed Indian wanted it.

But those piercing eyes cut through the crowded, smoky wharfside saloon and knocked Inigo Hull back on his heels and sent him tumbling back through nine years to that Wyoming mudhole. Blazing out of a sun-hammered gator-trapper's face, those unforgettable eyes had not yet spotted Hull, but worked their evil medicine on a hapless Dutchman who sucked at a clay pipe as he perused the map the old Indian was selling.

Hull sent his partner Dandy over to outbid the other worthy, who tugged his muttonchops and ran up the price like a medicine show barker's dupe. By the time Dandy yielded to the Dutchman, Hull had a bowie knife under the stranger's hairless chin, but the blue-eyed Indian only smiled wide enough for Hull to see his stolen teeth.

Dandy clubbed the stranger unconscious with his grayback cavalry saber. Nobody lifted a finger as Hull and Dandy blanketed the stranger in chains and dragged him to the jail. The sheriff let them stow their meat in a cell for a nominal handling charge while Hull wired Wichita. After he outdid the Devil with his promises and his deceits, they booked a stateroom on the next boat up the Mississippi.

His two partners each pitched their own fits: Dandy voted to send the Indian's head to Kansas in the post, and get back to whoring. Tom was hot to go west again, for reasons he would not make clear. They agreed that the treasure map was a fake and not worth a shit. Hull dared not tell them his reasons for wanting to follow the map, or for insisting on taking their prisoner upriver instead of overland, any more than he would tell them what he had heard back from the marshal's office in Kansas.

Hull had been riding with Tom the Prophet and Dandy Del Sur for almost two years, and toted up nearly twenty thousand dollars in bounties from the Dakota Territories to Chihuahua City. They worked well together, because neither of them hated redskins or had any sore sympathies over the Late Unpleasantness, and none nosed in the other's side business.

Tom the Prophet was a legendary tracker and gunslinger long before Hull was born. Even though his leathery hands shook like rattlers' tails, he could still shoot faster and straighter than any man alive.

Tom scarcely ever said a word on the trail, but he talked plenty in his cups. Hull knew that his real name was Elam Stroud. He rode down Mormon backsliders with Brigham Young's enforcers, the Angels of the Lord, until he began to hear his own angel. Hull figured this should have made him another Mormon holy man, but his angel was black and told him things that drove the Elders to exile him from Utah. He killed seventeen people there, including his own family, on the angel's orders. He had since sent another two hundred and ninety-two souls to somewhere that was neither Heaven nor Hell. The angel still spoke to him when a quarry or an ambush was close, or when some strange deed of its own needed doing. Afterward, in the lowest rut of a marathon drunk, Tom the Prophet talked back to his angel and all those he'd killed, whose souls he seemed to think burned somewhere deep inside him.

Dandy Del Sur seldom stopped talking about himself, but Hull knew nothing true about him, except that he had no real name.

Hull sent them off to the saloon to get loaded and took the hood off the stranger's head.

Their captive smiled at Hull, showing those three big white teeth, plugged in among his yellowed ones, etched with tiny geometric shapes that Hull knew must be the sacred writing of his tribe.

"What's your real name?"

"I am called Malakai, but I have also been Honest John and Prairie Puck and Reverend Walkaway, and I forget the rest. It is the gift of true wisdom to forget oneself. Why do you wear your hair so short? Do you really hope to pass for a white man?"

"Your tribe—what are they called, and where do they live?"

Delighted with this game, Malakai chuckled. "There's no one offering a bounty for our scalps, Hull. Not like your dear friends, the Comanche. You still grieve for them, though they threw you out. I only tried to show you what they truly were, you know: how fearful, how fragile and backward. Ah, but I am not answering your question, am I?"

"We came down from the stars with Great Tulu, before the land was divided from the sea. Bodiless, immortal, we mated with the animals called men and ruled the inner world from Hyperborea to the steppes of Kadath for as long as it pleased us. We are the Empire of Night; the Aggrieved Ones, the Ancient Enemy, the Seven Cities of K'n-yan. We are everywhere beneath you."

Tom the Prophet barged into the stateroom, roaring drunk and growling that the damned boat had nothing strong enough. Hull knew better than to order him out, so he ignored him and pressed on. "How long have you been killing travelers?"

"A foolish Spaniard called Zamacona opened the way when he came blundering into our homeland, searching for cities of gold and innocents to slaughter. But long before white men came, we were waiting."

Hull tried to remind himself he was not the one tied to a chair. He drained a shot of whiskey and tried to wipe the smile off the Indian's face. "You want war with the white man? Are you really so insane?"

"Since I am at your mercy, I will not lie to you. My people have wasted themselves in dreams and lost the will to give glory to the gods who sleep below. These greedy pale children rape the earth and spill blood so freely that their young nation is an altar, piled with sacrifices.

"But we are not savages, Inigo Hull. War is beneath us, and the white men are so very, very useful. We breed them with livestock, dissect them to divine the future, reawaken them to work or slaughter each other for our entertainment, and feed them to the gods of the gulf. But nothing is wasted . . . as with your buffalo."

"Be silent, warlock!" Tom the Prophet hurled an empty whiskey bottle at Malakai, but shattered a mirror above him instead. "The Angel has told me what you're about, and I have been charged to make you pay."

The blue-eyed Indian turned in his chains to grin at the Prophet. "A pity you're not welcome in Utah, Elam Stroud. There's a lovely valley I know, where the sweet spring falls from such a height that the air is alive with atomized water. We have a door behind those falls. Your Mormon children are so trusting, they can be plucked from the pasture there like ripe fruit, and so sweet, one can't help but devour them long before one could ever get them home . . ."

The Prophet launched a wild punch at Malakai, but Hull caught him and threw him back into his chair. The drunken gunslinger consoled himself by rifling through the Indian's black-beaded medicine bag. "Why's this damned thing so heavy? Where's your firewater, you God-blasted heathen cannibal?"

Dandy Del Sur swept into the room, drunk as a lord, but wearing it regally. "Señor Inigo," he slurred, "Dondy has heard stories of this blue-eyed Indian from many men who gave

Dondy all their money at faro table. They say he was hanged in Nacogdoches two years ago. His body turn to smoke and blow away. Another say this Indian was shot and burned in California, twenty years ago, but his ghost still haunt bottomless gold mine where hundreds gone missing. And another man who still is holding some of Dondy's money and his new woman, he tell Dondy he saw this blue-eyed Indian lynched in Idaho Falls just last summer. This bigmouth, he collect our bounty already."

"It was not the same man. This one killed a girl on an Army post in Wyoming and murdered hundreds on the Oregon Trail. Alive, he will be made to talk, lead the Army to his people."

Dandy Del Sur knew better than to call Hull a liar. "Dondy would rather apologize than argue." Dandy bowed deeply until the brim of his sombrero almost touched the floor. "Dondy is most humbly sorry."

Then he shot Malakai in the chest. The tiny silver snuffbox-pistol was a single-shooter, but it blew Malakai's heart out his back and pitched him backwards onto the deck.

"No more argument, eh?" Dandy left the cabin.

Tom the Prophet sat staring at Malakai's body. In his hand, quite forgotten, he held an onyx flask with an ornate silver cap carved in the shape of a snake's head.

Hull rushed over to check Malakai. The Indian's grin brimmed with blood. "Lord," he choked, "what fools these mortals be . . ." A single shrill whistle that seemed to skirl up beyond human hearing came from his lips, and he died.

"Amen," said Tom the Prophet and, popping the lid off the flask, took a deep swig from it.

Almost immediately he regretted it. Tom's eyes bugged out and he clutched his throat as if he meant to stop whatever he'd drank from getting to his gullet.

Curls of blue vapor streamed out his nose and around his

slack mouth. Hull knocked the flask from his hand, but Tom the Prophet shook like a man in a bad spell and dropped like a mailbag.

Hull poured his partner into a bed, but Tom bounced right back up and vomited far more fluid than he'd drunk tonight. Crawling after Hull with a hideously vacant grin, he sicked up a bottomless, steaming stew of melted gut rope. When he finally dropped dead on the last clean patch of floor in the stateroom, the poor bastard had more than halfway turned himself inside out.

The corpse of Elam Stroud lay petrified at Hull's feet for a long, pregnant moment before something stirred inside it.

Hull jumped back and drew his Colt. From the open mouth of the flask a steady stream of that insidious blue vapor dribbled out and snaked across the floor, drawn by some uncanny magnetism to flow into Tom the Prophet's gaping mouth.

Hull whirled and put two bullets into a stealthy creeping movement at the far end of the stateroom. He hit only the wall.

Malakai's body was gone. His chair lay upended on the floor, bloodied rags wreathed in empty chains. The same queer blue vapor oozed off the floor where his body had lain. It drifted away on the breeze out the open porthole.

Turning back to Tom the Prophet, Hull was stunned by the swift and sickening putrefaction of his corpse. Tom's gin-blossomed face was almost translucent, and as dry as a mummy's parchment flesh. As Hull reached out to drag the body from the room, the contorted, lipless mouth yawned wide until the whole head split like a cocoon, and something wet and red erupted from it.

A newborn man sat up out of the unmade bed of Tom's corpse and gave that same piercing whistle that was Malakai's death rattle. Hull shot three times and hit it once before the beaded bag on the floor came to life and filled the room with living, liquid darkness.

A shadow squirted up to the ceiling, then lashed out to snuff the gas jets on the walls, then the lantern, plunging the room into deepest shadow. Hull's last bullet passed right through it. He turned to see the newborn man crawl out of Tom's husk and roll away behind the settee before Hull could reload and shoot him.

Suddenly Hull was engulfed by a stygian blackness as solid as a wave of mud. A palpable, crushing shadow, it flung him effortlessly into the far wall. He collapsed on the floor like an empty suit of clothes.

Before Hull could catch his breath or draw a knife, it pounced on him again, its touch like cold entrails pinning him to the floor with the weight of a dead steer.

Naked, dripping, a resurrected Malakai crawled up close to Hull. "You should grow your hair longer." He took Hull's knife out of his belt. It came whistling out of the dark and hacked off both Hull's ears and disappeared again before he'd had a chance to hear the dreadful hiss of their removal.

"Be proud of what you are." Grimacing, Malakai stood and stretched his new body. He lifted an old black cloak out of Tom the Prophet's baggage and draped it over his shoulders.

Hull wept with pain and rage. He fought to breathe under the crushing bulk, struggling to rise to his feet the moment it had lifted itself.

"You know what you are," Malakai asked, "don't you?"

Hull hurled himself in the direction of the mocking voice, but he crashed through the open door and almost stumbled over the railing. Malakai was gone.

The Mississippi sparkled in the moonlight, bright as blue daylight after his ordeal in the stateroom.

Back near the paddlewheel, Dandy Del Sur leaned against the rail. Hull raced up to him, grabbing the rail to keep from falling more than once.

"Did you see him?"

Dandy Del Sur only shook his head a little, once.

"Dandy, *I* am the sorry one—"

Dandy Del Sur nodded his head once, and it fell off his shoulders and into the river.

March 15, 1900
River of Yoth

Even in a lost city of nightmares miles underground, Tobin Roherty was a man who always knew how to enjoy himself.

As his lackeys hogtied Inigo Hull, he loaded and lit up a meerschaum pipe, his alert left eye twinkling like Christmas, while the slanted right eye, cowled under its folds of scar tissue, glared hatefully at something only he could see.

Two of Cawthorne's runaway buck privates, Bledsoe and Parker, stood ready to shoot Hull if he cut loose. Bledsoe's unshaven, blue-jawed face was utterly blank with the shock of all he'd seen, while Parker, bug-eyed and bald as an egg, giggled and looked about him with giddy anticipation. Nobody bothered with Stickney after they searched him. The meek Indian agent was starting to come round. "Judas priest," Bledsoe scoffed. "He ain't even heeled!"

"I guess you know I don't give two shits about your Comanche cousins," Roherty allowed, "but I don't aim to go home empty-handed, either."

Hull slowly nodded his head. "You've heard the legends."

"Oh, we've all heard them, ain't we? The Indians told the Spaniards tall tales of golden cities to push them on over the next hill, and they ran themselves ragged trying to find them. Quivira, El Dorado, the Seven Cities of Cibola . . . I always knew they weren't just legends. Indians all know the truth, but they're afraid to tell, with a fear thousands of years older than them, of something they don't even understand. But that fear don't come to much when you've got their guts in your hands."

"The houses of Tsath are built of gold and silver. You could pick it up off the ground like trash."

"Well, I could indeed, but if gold is trash to them, a man must get to thinking, what do they keep for treasure?"

Hull just looked intently at Roherty. The scarred scalp-hunter puffed at his pipe, lost in thought. He looked, more than anything, like a baby passing wind.

Hull nodded at his throat and shrugged until a pendant on a leather thong around his neck slipped out of his coat and dangled before him. A dull, blue-gray metal, it twisted on the thong and swayed unnervingly when Hull moved, as if drawn to something like a magnet to its own secret pole. "This metal fell from the stars, and there is only a little of it in all the world. Like calls to like, so they cast their idols of Yig and Tulu in it, and use these coins to be led to worship."

"That's not exactly what I meant. You know . . ." Roherty's lively eye went vague and runny, like his slack one, as if he'd lost his thought, and searched for it in Hull's impassive copper face. "Shiny stuff . . ."

Motionless, face streaming sweat, Hull poured all his will out through his eyes. "You know what they prize above all things."

Roherty blinked, then grinned wickedly. "I do, at that. Diamonds, but not just little trinket-stones. They use them to work their big medicine, and they're so precious, they don't keep them in the city. They keep them hid away in a place even they're afraid to go to . . . down yonder, on this very river."

Hull sagged with relief. "You seem to know more about it than I do."

Roherty just stared at Hull, as if he was somehow being hoodwinked. He leaned forward and ripped the strange pendant from Hull's neck. "You'll lead me to it."

"You don't need us. That coin will lead you."

"Maybe it will, and maybe it won't. But I don't plan to go in half-cocked. But what's got me buffaloed is; how've they kept hidden for so long?"

"It is their way to cloud men's minds, the better to lead them to their deaths. For as long as your kind have been conquering and taming the land above, they have moved among you as cowboys, driving their cattle to slaughter."

Roherty pursed his lips and sprayed his contempt. "Bullshit! This is the United States of America, not the goddamned Congo! Someone must have known they were down here—"

"Someone *has* always known," Hull calmly replied. "Even the Indians who have forgotten the old ways and embraced the cross know in their hearts that Hell is a very real, living place, just beneath their feet. But no one ever asked the Indian what he believed. No one ever asked for anything but his land and his life."

"That's right tragic," Roherty said. "I humbly wish to apologize on behalf of my dastardly white ancestors for fuckin' up your little Paradise. But this ol' world is a pie-eating contest, old-timer, and Devil take the hindmost. You don't finish yours quick enough, somebody's apt to take it, and that's just the way the Great Spirit wants it, or why else would it be so?"

Stickney, who was sitting up again, tried to engage Roherty in debate, but Private Parker clubbed his jewels with his rifle butt.

Roherty relit his pipe. "So these cowardly bushwhackers have been hunting white folks for sport since powder-wig days. Why're they comin' after *your* kinfolk, all of a sudden?"

Hull bridled at the claim of kinship with the Comanche, but he ironed the furrows out of his brow before he spoke. "K'n-yan cut itself off from the outer world ages ago, and would have faded away, but for Malakai. He hungers to revive the most terrible of the Great Old ones of N'kai: the one called He-Who-Sleeps-Beneath-Us, or Tsathoggua. Even his mad brothers in the Seven Cities would not suffer the terrible changes required to open the eye of the dreaming toad-god, but there are many all over America who would give their blood and their children's souls to see the white man wiped away once and for all. To see his cities drowned in blood, they would give all they have left—"

"Don't make no never-mind to me if the redskins want to worship a toad, or the Man in the goddamn Moon. I don't want their gods, just their loot."

"Do you believe in God, Mr. Roherty?"

"What the hell kind of question is that? Course I do."

"And yet you know you will pay in Hell for all the evil that you've done. Your God is something to comfort you in the darkness. But for the sake of your soul, He must not be real. There are beings beneath the earth, and under the sea, and in the dark between the stars, who are older than the earth and yet alive, made of immortal star-stuff, but very real. What else could one call them, Mr. Roherty, but gods? What could one do, when facing their awful undying medicine, but kneel and pray to be spared?"

Tobin Roherty scratched at the scar that split his face, and shivered, shaking with nasty hilarity. "*Oh, Lord, help me, I'm so scared!* Boys, are you scared?"

Parker and Bledsoe had all but polished off the last of the expedition's whiskey and feared nothing.

Hull pressed on. "The man who led the Comanche bands down here has brought them to face the bottomless abyss where Tsathoggua sleeps. They will dance the Backward Path and sacrifice until he awakens. Indian Territory will catch fire with the new faith, and the nation will descend into a second civil war . . . against the land itself."

"Well shit, I wouldn't want to be anywhere near that mess," said Roherty. "And thanks to your Uncle Tobin, neither will you." He leapt up onto the prow of the galley and held out Hull's coin on its plumbline. "Run us aground up yonder!"

The inky gloom of the riverine cavern had given way to a morbid red glow suffused with sulfurous steam. The air became sultry and stagnant, and steeped in a sour reek like mildew and mold.

Out of the crimson fog came a ragged shore strewn with massive boulders in staggered lines suggesting the collapsed pillars of some insanely vast structure.

Beyond the ruinous shore, a dim skyline of Cyclopean pyramids and toppled towers reached up to penetrate the distant roof of the grotto. This impossibly ancient city dwarfed its blue-lit neighbor Tsath, but it was also far more alien.

Hull finally relented to Stickney's needling questions. "The men of Tsath settled in the caverns above because they were drawn to the ruins of an older race that rose and fell long before the great thunder lizards died out. It was on their plundered graves that K'n-yan built their greatest inventions. Their dreaming engines spun matter out of pure energy, and stored souls could fly to new bodies or live forever in their crystal prisms. This is what you're looking for, Roherty. But if we don't go down to N'kai now, you'll have no place above ground to spend your fortune."

Roherty advanced on Hull with one of his own bowie knives and raised it as if to scalp the half-breed bounty hunter, making his lackeys laugh. He brushed back Hull's hair and tsked at the ugly knots of scar tissue where his ears once were. "Someone beat me to it," he sighed. He cut Hull's bonds and gave him back his Navy revolver.

The galley lurched to a halt on the rocks. Nobody rushed to jump off. The *y'm-bhi* sat silently at their oars. "All ashore, you maggots!" Roherty shoved Hull over the gunwale, but he landed on his bootheels. Parker shoved the pack mules over the edge into the brackish black shallows, and Bledsoe dragged them out. Roherty kicked the Indian agent overboard, then jumped after and waded ashore.

The city of Yoth was indeed a wonder to behold, but only the highest of its crumbling basalt spires rose above the sunless jungle that had infested the abandoned hothouse grotto. Gargantuan white trees greater than redwoods loomed over them and blocked out all but thin rays of the lurid scarlet light. As they came nearer, they found that the jungle was a riotous plague of grotesque subterranean fungus.

Huge, drooping canopies of mutant mushrooms sprinkled clouds of spores like snow flurries from their pulsing gills as they trudged among the rubble of Yoth. They detoured around monstrous puffballs and undulating fields of slime mold, and curtains of quivering tendrils dangling to ensnare the blind white moth-things that swooped and ignited themselves on their torches. They wrapped bandanas over their faces to filter out the overpowering miasma of the fungal rainforest, which only worsened as they pressed closer to the city center.

"How much further?" Stickney tried not to whine, but he could barely breathe through his sodden handkerchief. "I'm near done in, but . . . I can manage . . . if I have to . . ."

"There is a well at the city's center," Hull said. "The stairs descend for almost a mile, to the temple over the black gulf."

"But we're not going there, are we?" Roherty called a halt and looked around the city with Hull's weird coin out in one hand and a lost look, as if trying to recall a dream. "That one." He pointed at a hexagonal tower that pierced the roof of the cavern, a mile in the opposite direction from the city center. "You play along, Hull, and maybe you'll walk out of this a rich half-breed. What the hell is that?"

They had stopped in a broad, fractured plaza where a huge fault line had swallowed half of a pyramid. The eroded paving stones rippled and ranks of freestanding basalt columns tilted and fell over as something huge passed beneath them.

Parker was complaining about his rifle and angling for Roherty to give him Hull's Sharps gun, when he stepped in something. "Tarnation! Boys, I do believe I jus' struck oil!"

He lifted his boot off the octagonal paving stones, but a thick, viscous rope of black slime clung to it, stubbornly holding his boot fast to a crack in the ground. More of the stuff oozed out of the crack with the suet-slippery consistency of blood pudding.

"Help me out here, boys," Parker said as the gusher streamed up his leg, "and I'll cut you all in for a share."

Bledsoe reached out to grab his friend. Hull said, "Wait," but it was too late.

A torrent of glistening black slime exploded out of the crack. Flailing pseudopod clubs and flytrap tentacles wrapped Parker up and dragged back down into the crack, crushing him to pulp within itself as it went. The others could only try to shoot Parker dead before his howling, pulverized remains were sucked out of sight.

"Run!" Hull cried. Roherty climbed onto the base of a splintered obelisk and stuffed his pipe. Bledsoe and the mules turned tail without another thought, but Stickney stood rooted to the spot, even as he wet himself.

The paving stones split asunder and were flung like grenade shrapnel across the plaza. The ground subsided and gave way before them as the full bulk of the formless monstrosity burst into view.

A pulsating column of molten hunger rose up out of the fissure and bristled with trembling cilia, greedily scenting the air for the nearest prey.

Hull raised his revolver and fired into the quivering mass. It recoiled more in surprise than pain, but then sprouted hundreds of blunt, churning legs and flowed across the plaza after him like an enormous millipede.

Hull shouted "Run!" once more at Stickney. He stood dead in the path of the oncoming monstrosity, but he did not raise his gun to it. Instead, he uttered a quavering whistle that seemed to start somewhere in his boots, but swiftly climbed right up out of hearing range. He could still feel it in his sinuses, and so, apparently, could the monster.

Rearing up and coiling back on itself in agitation like a mass of animate blubber or a vast, landlocked octopus, it writhed away from the hurtful sound and hastened back respectfully when Hull stepped toward it.

"God damn," Roherty said, "is there no godforsaken creature these redskins can't tame?" He stood right beside a still paralyzed Stickney. The Indian agent couldn't see him, but he saw the long, heavy barrel of Hull's fifty-caliber buffalo rifle rise up and discharge a blast that ruptured Stickney's right eardrum.

Hull's head from the ears up turned into red confetti. The fount of gore sprayed the prostrate abomination and provoked it to a berserker fury. A frothy black wave towered over Inigo Hull's half-headless corpse even as the bounty hunter spun on its heel by dead reflex and drew on Tobin Roherty.

His twelve-shot Navy revolver hammered the paving stones before and beside the scarfaced scalp-hunter. It sparked twice more inside the collapsing tube of the black wave that swiftly and silently enveloped him, and then the formless monstrosity flattened Hull and swiftly digested him.

"Dear God," Stickney moaned. "You shot him in the back, you . . . you . . ."

Roherty pointed the rifle at Stickney's head. "Don't make me waste a bullet on you, boy."

To his everlasting shame, Stickney didn't.

Roherty lit the fuse of a stick of dynamite off his pipe and tossed it at the raging black wave cresting again to come for them. "If you see any more of them noble savages about, Mr. Indian Agent, I hope you'll politely ask them to direct you to the exit. You know how well kindness civilizes the savages."

The dynamite went off inside the oncoming black wave and was expelled in a clump of bubbles, but hardly slowed it down. Stickney climbed up onto a toppled obelisk and watched the black protoplasm chase Roherty off into the depths of the fungus jungle. Unnoticed, he lay against the stone until the booming of dynamite and the screams of animals and men had died down to a whisper of an echo.

No water, no food, no weapons. If he stayed here, no doubt he would die before he got thirsty. He was the only survivor of the expedition who had not abandoned its mission.

The place Hull had been leading them to, if any of this was to be believed, was where the Comanche had gone with that man who had led them out from under his care. They were his responsibility. He could not kill this Malakai, or kill anyone, but he could try to stop it. He would do something, with or without the government's help, for these poor, broken people he had fallen in love with in books, but had come to despise in the flesh. And he would almost certainly die, unknown, unremembered, miles beneath the surface of the earth. Or he could turn around, and go home . . .

But I don't know the way home, he told himself, over and over. *And I am so tired . . .and this is probably closer than home, anyway . . .*

Hull could see only blue light, which bothered him, because he had no eyes. He could feel no warmth or cold, or anything else, for he had no hands or body with which to feel anything.

The only solution to the riddle was that he *was* the blue light. And yet, this was not the sky . . . and certainly not Heaven. And only then, did he remember . . .

He was fighting the K'n-yan—foolish, for they risked nothing and attacked him only for sport. One of them must have killed him, and this was a dream—

No, he sourly realized. The soothing azure light pulsed with a powerful mechanical rhythm, and as his 'eyes' adjusted, he saw waves in the infinite blue field that gave hints of others, swimming in this infinite sea.

The last thing he remembered was the whining chain-blade of a rotary dagger biting into his back when he shot the second of the three warriors who ambushed him. They must have killed him there and somehow made him one of them.

Now, Malakai had finally won.

If he had simply died, it would be over. Malakai could keep coming back forever, but now so could he.

Hull reflected on all the other times he'd tracked, caught, and killed the blue-eyed Indian. All the other times he'd believed he'd finished it. And all the other times that he'd missed him.

In 1883, the Gotha Silver Mine opened and soon became the rowdiest of the Colorado boomtowns. The miners worked its rich silver veins on a unique profit-sharing basis that shamed the other company towns. Three hundred and fifty men worked the Gotha mine until a series of suspicious cave-ins buried more than half of them in three days. When too many miners never returned, the survivors went on strike, and there was a riot. A short time later (but it wasn't a short time later, it was the morning after the riot) the entire town vanished over-night—miners, whores—leaving uneaten food on plates and unfinished drinks standing on the saloon bar. Not until he saw a Wanted poster for the company president, Adolf Gotha, did Hull suspect how good Malakai was at the game. For in the end, that was all it was to the K'n-yan medicine man.

In Tolerance, ten years ago, Hull thought he'd finally won. The buried town had rested on a honeycomb of tunnels that eventually led to the lost K'n-yan city of Kyuss. After killing Malakai in the lava tubes and again in the half-abandoned ruin, the truth dawned on him. Captain Boyer was a brave officer and a decent man, and he'd brought dynamite. After all hope of escape was lost, they'd dropped the cavern roof on half the city, and the nauseous flood of blue mist gushing from the temples had been stopped. Malakai did not return again. Among the ru-ins he'd found the map of gold and rubies set in the basalt floor of the central plaza, and learned that there were six other cities.

Now he was an eternal part of their mad, empty game. It was his fate to chase Malakai until he became him. He had learned from the Union Army that one must embrace the worst of one's enemy to defeat him, but one could only be half as cruel as an enemy and still win with honor. He had led Major Cawthorne and his men down here to use them, just as Malakai meant to use the Comanche to serve his own ends.

He could forsake the empty game. He could retreat into the mist and never take on a body. They couldn't force him, could they? He could lie in wait until K'n-yan and the white men and the Indians destroyed each other, and if the hunting then was still no good, he'd go back to sleep forever.

But the idea of existing in limbo without a body was worse than hell. Oblivion would be its own reward, but his sense of purpose was not a gland in his body. It still dug at him that he'd failed to stop Malakai for good. It ate at him that he'd worked for the men who exterminated his people and he had never done anything to save them; out of a child's spite at being cast out so long ago, he could barely remember what it felt like.

The people of K'n-yan could die and return in new bodies at their whim, so he could do the same. And even if he was trapped in limbo, he could still find some way to make them wish to be rid of him.

And his people were still somewhere below, if Malakai hadn't already fed them to the abyss.

Welcome home, Inigo Hull, Malakai whispered in his mind. Hull threw up an imaginary shield against the intruder, but he could 'see' only a weird trailing wake, like the shape of a tall man, in the blue blizzard. His ancient enemy was all around him, but he couldn't touch him.

Searching again, he saw a faded quadrant of the azure void grow dim and fade to a dead, dull black. Tiny cracks fanned out like capillaries from the dead space, throbbed and swelled into arteries shooting through the empty blue ocean of the dreaming engines.

A dreadful sound that was not a sound boomed throughout the infinite blue dream, and a thunderous voice roared from everywhere at once. "GOD DAMN YOU, INIGO HULL, I

CURSE YOUR NAME, YOU BACKSTABBING HALF-BREED COCKSUCKER!"

By the sound of it, Tobin Roherty had found the Yothic dreaming engines and mistaken the huge crystal dream-lenses for diamonds. But when Hull sent the bounty hunter to wreck the dreaming engines, he never imagined that he would be trapped inside them.

Hull cast about for an exit, and the very thought seemed to make it manifest itself. Ahead lay a yawning white whirlpool, but Malakai's ghost floated before and behind him and whispered so loudly that his voice rang the void like a tuning fork. *It's time you knew the truth about your people.*

September 28, 1851
Red Crow Mound, Kansas

A decorated officer, the son of a war hero, and the great grandson of a brigadier general, yet Lieutenant Cadmus Hull would have thrown away his command and run away that night for her.

His detachment of eight cavalry troopers and a Pawnee scout had been three days on the trail of a party of Comanche renegades who raided a homestead on the Texas border, when they became lost on the prairie. The stars failed to come out at night, and the moon never rose. The men grumbled that he was leading them in circles.

This was no place for a West Point–educated horse officer. This vast green sea of grass should have been the Navy's responsibility to defend, but he had fallen head over heels in love with it. After the stifling warrens of Baltimore and the humiliating crush of Army life, the Great Plains had unchained his heart and filled him with strange ambitions.

The emptiness was like a subtle sign, a mute mandate, from

God. When everything around it was so abundantly blessed and lovingly shaped by the Creator's hand, the prairie beckoned to Hull's mind because it seemed as if God had left it so conspicuously blank for man to try his own hand at creation. When Cadmus Hull looked at the plains, he saw a vast city and dreamed of his hand in its rearing, his name on its streets.

America was almost exactly half-tamed. All but a few stubborn holdouts among the native population had moved out of the east and south, but the endless plains and the Great Desert were something else again. The Sioux, Cheyenne, Comanche, and Apache showed what one had to become to thrive in such a wasteland. But it was an animal's lot to conform to the dictates of the land. A white man brought the country to heel and made it yield its bounty.

They'd ridden since dusk, six hours without seeing the rally point, or any landmark, elevation, or sign of life since the stampeding herd of buffalo that had driven them off the trail. The men argued among themselves about which direction they were headed, but agreed in loud mutterings that Hull was leading them to slaughter.

They'd passed abandoned homesteads with crops overripe in the fields, and wagon trains with grass woven through the spokes of broken wheels. There were no bodies or possessions and no signs of violence, as if the settlers had just set out for somewhere better on foot.

When Hull saw the pinpoint of orange light on the horizon, twinkling just above a lonely hill in the midst of the grassy nothingness, he thought it was a star. But it grew larger and brighter, beckoning him closer, until he galloped up the steep slope and found himself in the midst of the fugitive Comanche camp.

Hull drew his pistol and shouted an alarm, but the warriors

lay prone upon black-red beds of bloody earth. The beacon that led him here was a torch in a woman's hand.

No, he corrected himself with his second glance—a lady. Even from a distance, something in her bearing and her simple garments commanded his respect, even as the wild, pleading panic in her eyes inspired him to protect her.

He thought at first she was white, for she was so fair, but her black hair and almond-shaped, indigo eyes hinted at an exotic origin, perhaps Celestial. If she was an Indian, she was like none he'd ever seen. Whatever she was and wherever she came from, Hull knew she must be royalty.

She wailed in a strange tongue and dropped her torch as he approached, but she didn't run away. Lieutenant Hull sent the others to encircle the mound, while he jumped down and quite instinctively took her in his arms.

The seven Comanche braves had not built a fire, but someone had come upon them in the night and quietly killed them. Only one of the men had been eaten, but all had been opened up and disemboweled where they slept on the ground. They lay in a circle around a lump of green-black stone crudely carved into the shape of a squat toad with a wizened face and mocking, sleepy smile. Lieutenant Hull was not a religious or superstitious man, but a powerful revulsion stole into his bones at the touch of that blood-flecked idol, and he still felt its sickly weight and warmth in his hand long after he threw it into the dark.

She spoke no English, but the lady made herself understood with signs and meaningful glances that somehow told him more than words. Her own people had cast her out, and she had been taken by the Comanche war party only a few days before. They had tied her up and argued among themselves over which of them would have her, when something had come out of the night and slaughtered them all. She did not know why she was spared, but when it had left she had lit a fire to try to signal for help.

Lieutenant Hull lifted her up on his horse. She rode with easy, weightless grace, clinging lightly to his back when he galloped after his men. The scout with their party told them that if they camped anywhere near the massacred Comanche on the "hollow hill," they would wake up in Hell.

They camped an hour to the south, beside a winding creek on none of Hull's maps. Hull led the lady he'd saved down by the water and gave her a ring he'd inherited from his mother when she died penniless in Baltimore. She told him her name.

The troopers broke camp before dawn. Hull and his woman were the last to rise. Only then did they set out.

Somewhere over the hills just breaching on the southern horizon, Major General Maddox was completing his spring cleaning of the Texas panhandle. He was expecting them back with news of swift American retribution on the Comanche.

Hull stopped his procession of cavalry troopers again beside a lazy river, despite the protests of his men. They were a day's ride from the company. But they'd complained about riding all night into southern Kansas, and he didn't let them forget it. One wiseacre among the men had learned that his ancestor, General William Hull, had surrendered to Tecumseh in the War of 1812, and now his chronic cough had always sounded peculiarly like the old chief's name. Now, he croaked worse accusations into his fist.

But Lieutenant Hull blithely put all this out of his mind when he took the lady by the hand into the long grass at sunset. They lay together by the gurgling current, and he told her about the great cities in the east and the strange nations beyond the sea. She was almost as eager for these stories as for his other attentions, but he lusted even more to lose himself in those boundless, unblinking eyes that seemed to peel away all his secrets and accept him.

They lay entwined on the grass when the men came and tried to take her. The jealous Pawnee scout filled their heads with stories. She was not an Indian of the Plains, but a shadow woman of the Unseen Empire. She had killed the Comanche herself, and she would do the same to them. She had bewitched their commander, but they would do their duty.

They tried to string her up. Hull shot two of his own men dead and held the rest at bay, then rode off with her, headed west.

They lived together in a draw off Apache Creek, far from the trails. Fed by a spring and with arable land for raising crops, they were happy for some months, until the Comanche came.

Cadmus Hull was shot through with nine arrows when he reached their cabin. His wife was heavy with their child, and they caught her. By the time they brought her back to their camp, three braves were already competing for her attentions. When she delivered her child, she would have her pick of the finest of the Kotsotekas braves.

But on the day she delivered her baby, she died, and some said she went up to the sky in a cloud of blue smoke, leaving the oddly quiet, green-eyed half-breed child in their midst. They raised him as Comanche, but knew he was different, for when he slept, Inigo Hull lay face down, with his arms out to embrace the earth.

March 16, 1900
Gulf of N'kai

As Oliver Stickney ran through the twisting avenues and fungi-fields of Yoth, he wished to be anywhere else, even back in the haunted purgatory of Tsath, rather than alone in this unhinged Inferno.

The bas-reliefs and leering idols everywhere, overhead and underfoot, were more intensely vivid and obscene than those of the blue-lit ruins above, but also far more alien. These decorations were as if the decadent artisans of K'n-yan labored to express their adoration for serpentine and octopoid motifs, or that the insane builders of Yoth had been serpents themselves. And the objects of their devotion were too terrible to bear closer study.

The monstrous mushroom trees had succumbed to legions of withering parasitic fungi in this district, and the central plaza was open to the artificial sky. Clusters of dusky, deeply flawed ruby globes hung from the lofty, vaulted ceiling to light the city-sized cavern and bathe it in fertile heat and humidity.

A circular hole, sixty or so feet across, yawned in the center of the ruined city. The walls of the flanking pyramids were scabbed with fleshy white fungi-like cancerous cauliflower. Deep, opaque shadows crept and stretched across the plaza around him, as if the artificial sun raced through the sky overhead . . .

Squirming wads of black protoplasm dragged themselves over the broken ground and streaked down the sloping pyramid walls to surround him. For all their hideous kinship to the oldest single-celled life on earth—the amoeba—yet they betrayed a shrewd predatory cunning that more than matched his own.

Primal fear and panic warred with a raging disgust in his trembling chest. His best efforts wouldn't keep them at bay, yet they never closed in for the kill. He was not being stalked. He was being herded.

At the edge of the pit Stickney sorely wished for a gun, though he knew how little good it would do. Peering nervously over the sheer wall, he saw a narrow staircase winding down the inside of the pit.

Though the formless horde reared up at his heels, Stickney balked on the top step at the faint echoes of a man's voice from somewhere far below. He recognized the voice, but even here in this place it gave him no comfort to hear the cries of Major Cawthorne, roaring in wordless grief and rage.

The stairs were slick and badly eroded by water seepage and eons of inhuman feet. The carvings lining the walls of the pit became mercifully unclear in the deepening gloom, but under his groping hands the lurid animal motifs devolved in an orgy of miscegenation: blasphemous couplings of bat, serpent, toad, and octopus begat and bred with their own mutant offspring. And as he descended, the misbegotten forms devolved into a uniform, plastic formlessness that he could not bear to touch any longer.

The echoing bedlam from down below gradually resolved into clearer impressions. He still heard the unhinged bellowing of the expedition commander, but wafting on the fetid, frigid breeze, he also heard the low rumbling of hundreds of voices chanting that strange, terrible name: *Sadogwa*.

And behind him he heard a stealthy sound that was neither dripping fluid, nor the padding of creeping feet, but something in between . . .

He descended more urgently now, passing his hand quickly over the hideously carven walls, but he stopped and quashed a scream in the back of his throat when his hand slipped from cold, chiseled stone and brushed hot, sweating flesh.

"Please, don't kill me . . ." the face in the dark begged him. "I can't go on . . . He's gone mad. He led us . . . but they . . . those things . . . they herded us down here! I was just following his orders, but he shot the others . . . I just . . . I want to go home."

Fighting his own craven panic, Stickney grabbed the man's woolen shoulders and shook him. He felt a lieutenant's braided boards under his fingers. "Get a hold of yourself, for God's sake! You're supposed to be a soldier ..." The officer was not wounded, just hysterical from all he had seen and survived.

Stickney touched the lieutenant's holster and took his pistol. The man didn't resist, and he didn't listen to Stickney's warning that it wasn't safe up the stairs. The deserter bolted up the spiraling flight in a gibbering panic. Somewhere above, he screamed once, then fell instantly silent.

Stickney plunged down the remaining coils of the stairway in a dead panic. When he finally stumbled out onto the level floor of a natural tunnel, he wanted to fall down and kiss it, but the flickering light that lured him out of the tunnel lifted him to his feet and brought him running.

He emerged in a wide, low-roofed cave. A low, ancient step pyramid reached halfway to the low ceiling, and at its base a great bonfire burned.

After uncounted hours in total darkness or under the unnatural illumination of the caverns of Yoth and Tsath, the honest light of a bonfire should have been a comfort, a beacon of sanity. But the firelight was broken up by the leaping silhouettes of dozens of dancing men, women, and children, and scores more sat or lay prone on the steps, spent and desolate as lightning-struck trees. His heart broke as he finally found the people he had come down into hell to save.

They danced and chanted like sleepwalkers in a loose, shambling procession around and over the pyramid as he passed among them. Stickney had observed with real interest the dances of the various tribes who were unwilling neighbors in the Oklahoma Indian Territory, and he'd been touched by their grace and intricate symbolism. But this debased ritual was a travesty of the Indian and all he believed, and of the human form itself.

Locked in a deep, frenzied trance that urged them beyond the limits of their bodies, they looked right through him as they cavorted and abused themselves and each other with spastic blows from fist, nails, and feet. Painted from head to toe in stinking black filth, they jumped like broken-winged bats and crawled on the stones like toads, and in the guttering light of a noisome bonfire fed with piles of dried fungi, the bad medicine of this unholy place seemed close to granting their wish.

Severed once and for all from their sacred bond to the land, the Comanche seemed to pray to the void to let them shed their human skins and slip into the shrinking wilderness and fall into shadow. And everything that walked on two legs would be swept away by what they hoped to awaken.

Huge, hairless, deformed bats soared in out of the dark to add their flailing wings to the flames, or to latch onto oblivious Indians and glut themselves on their blood.

One renegade dancer capered to his own tune, running amok with a cavalry saber and an empty pistol. Howling "Stop this abomination, you godless red bastards!" he lopped the head and arms off an ancient naked man, but the dolorous strokes threw him to his knees.

Major Cawthorne was drenched in blood and foaming at the mouth. Dismembered corpses and orphaned limbs lay scattered in his wake. He had spent himself in wanton killing without even getting the dancers' attention. Indeed, he seemed to be a critical ingredient in the dehumanizing ritual.

Stickney climbed halfway up the pyramid, searching the chaos for the blue-eyed Indian Hull had called Malakai. He saw him on a towering altar that loomed at the summit of the pyramid.

Naked and gleaming blue in the cold cobalt light of an

atomic lantern, Malakai performed a strange dance as subdued and subtle as the Comanche dance was bestial and depraved. His face wracked with silent invocation, his hands stretched out to the abyss and beckoning to something that waited below.

At his back, a squat green-black idol loomed over the empty altar. Stickney recognized it for a twin of the weathered stone atop White Widow Mound. He understood just as quickly, why someone had defaced its features, to hide its true face.

The bloated body of a toad sprawled over the edges of the dais. Its shaggy head was that of a bat, with gnarled, veiny ears cocked as if to hear the merest whisper of its nauseous name. Great goggling eyes with heavy, drooping lids stared down at the depraved orgy with sardonic amusement, as if all the madness and atrocities were but a sweet, fleeting dream.

This was the unthinkable thing the reptilian race that reared Yoth had worshipped, until their blessed extinction; the sleeping deity whose dreams had led the people of K'n-yan to madness; the abominable demon the blue-eyed Indian had brought to his reservation.

This had to be stopped. Inigo Hull had given his life trying to stop it, only to be shot in the back with his own gun by that scum Tobin Roherty . . .

There was no one else. He looked around for Major Cawthorne, but saw no one—

"*Traitor!*" the drawn-out, wounded cry came from just behind him. Stickney whirled around, the unfamiliar bulk of the .45 Colt slippery in his shaky hand, but the curved saber at his throat and the gun barrel in his back ran any fanciful dreams of action right out of his mind.

Cawthorne seethed in his ear. "You abandoned us, boy. You and that gutless prairie-nigger bounty hunter left us to die—"

"No, Major, it wasn't like that! Hull was right, and we were wrong! You were—"

"Shut your yellow hole, you goddamned renegade!" Cawthorne smashed him in the mouth with the butt of his pistol. Stickney dropped quickly, then Cawthorne kicked him where he lay. "This is why they must be exterminated and swept away, root and branch! Behind their subhuman masks, they're animals or worse! Their way of life is a disease, and you've become infected, Mr. Stickney—"

Despite his wounds, Stickney rolled over and raised the gun, pulled the trigger with his eyes closed and shot Major Cawthorne in the throat, then hammered him three more times before he hit the ground.

Spooked flocks of vampire bats shrieked and took wing, flapping back into the bottomless gulf. The endless dance of devolution continued around the Indian agent. On his perch at the summit, Malakai clapped and shouted, "It feels good, doesn't it?"

Stickney numbly levered himself upright and stepped over Cawthorne's corpse, staggering towards the high altar, when he got his first glimpse of the cavern beyond the pyramid. Stickney's head swam and his stomach rolled when he looked out into it and saw nothing at all, forever.

The irregular edge of the chasm cut across the far corner of the step pyramid, and Stickney realized with sickly certainty that the whole pyramid lay upon a shelf thrust far out over the void. The ribbed roof of the cave gave way, likewise, to a perfect blackness teeming with flapping, chittering nightmares.

The floor beneath them sagged and swayed in sympathy with every rolling impact of the tribe's feet and fists pounding upon the crumbling basalt bricks. If they only beat the earth with their bodies a little harder, and in rhythmic unison, the ledge beneath them would surely collapse into the bottomless gulf of N'kai.

He forced his eyes back down to the ground before his feet. The gun was much lighter in his hand. He pointed it and squeezed off a warning shot. "Malakai—or whatever you call yourself! Release your claim upon these people forthwith!"

Malakai regarded him with a short bark of sneering laughter. "Will you release them as well? Did you not drive them from their homes and drop them at my door? Did you not starve them in summer and leave them to freeze in winter, and quietly murder their way of life? I did not take them, little man. You delivered them to me. You sent them on the Backward Path. And look, I have answered their prayers."

All about the pyramid the Comanche lurched on in their dreadful dance, but their faltering steps grew elastic and fluid, swimming through the air as if through molasses, and their bodies began to change.

Arms and legs bowed and warped under their weight, as if their bones were becoming soft, rotting or melting inside them. Some among the mob writhed on the basalt steps, wracked with convulsions and spraying foam from impossibly stretching mouths as they vomited forth, bone by painful bone, their own skeletons. Stickney bit back bile and clawed at his skull to hold in his sanity as those boneless bodies rose up again to slither the Backward Path in a monstrous imitation of Tsathoggua's formless offspring.

Such things could not be, and yet he saw them. He could not stand to see any more, but perhaps he could stop it.

Stickney sighted down the big steeple on the end of the Colt's barrel and shot the priest.

Malakai didn't even flinch as the bullet passed through his chest. "We are all Nature's instruments, white man. The world is a game playing itself. But you are not the proper instrument, for my deliverance."

Stickney came closer. The liquid shadows at the base of the altar quivered and drew erect and raked the air with branching, barbed pseudopods. Swimming in sweat and goosebumps, he fired again.

Malakai twisted and let the bullet cleave the air beside his face. "I will die tonight, but I prefer to be killed by a knife. I would suffer you to bear witness, but don't try my patience. Where is Inigo Hull?"

Oh God, he doesn't know, Stickney thought. And instantly, Malakai *did* know.

Lifting a long, tapered dagger, he slashed the air and leapt down from the altar. "You monstrous, bloodthirsty, vain, greedy, hollow *fools!* You could not even be trusted to bring him to me!"

Stickney jumped back and turned his face away as he emptied the gun at Malakai.

When he turned to look at what he'd shot, a flying torrent of black slime engulfed the gun and swallowed his hand up to the wrist. When he pulled it back, the gun was gone and so, down to the smoking bone, was his hand.

Stickney sank sobbing to his knees, cradling the cauterized stump. Malakai stood over him. "If you are so intent on being useful, you can fall on this knife or throw yourself into the pit."

Stickney closed his eyes. A chill, damp sensation enveloped him. He must be going into shock. When he opened them again, he saw only clouds of blue mist pouring up the pyramid steps to converge on Malakai's perch.

"You are welcome to watch, my brothers and cousins," the high priest sneered, "but if you would stand between K'n-yan and its rebirth to glory, then I will add your poison souls to the sacrifice."

The blue mist eddied and swarmed and clotted around a

pillar, stout and suddenly quite solid. The pillar raised its arms and shook itself, then waved away the mists, which retreated like whipped dogs from the resurrected man.

Stickney hid his head, then looked up and whimpered, "It can't be . . . I saw you die . . ."

"I was not allowed to," said Inigo Hull. His hair was still the color of steel dust, but the wrinkles in his face and the stooped weariness in his carriage had been ironed out of his rawboned, powerful form.

A cold, noxious wind blew up from the mouth of the pit. Hull's hair flew back from his head, laying bare his missing ears.

Malakai laughed. "Excellent! Now you are truly one of us, my son! But you could have restored your ears and teeth. Will you always see yourself as maimed?"

"You did not give me these scars," Hull replied. "I earned them."

"And you know, at last, why you were always so precious to me. I gave my only daughter to the outer world, but the world gave you to me. And all for what must be done tonight."

Hull drew his coffin-handled knives from their sheaths and held them up to catch both the yellow glow of the fire and the blue glow of the atomic lantern. Any shock he might have felt at the revelation he shrugged it off with a grim and mirthless smile. "I've only ever wanted one thing from you, old man. Nothing between us has changed."

Malakai stepped closer to Hull, who seemed paralyzed, or even—Stickney felt sick at the thought—a trick of the damnable blue mist, and not the real Hull, at all.

"Perfect!" Malakai cried. "I had hoped you would bring a knife."

Malakai jumped back as Hull surged after him, hacking the air in audible arcs with his bloodthirsty knives. The high priest climbed back onto the altar and took up his own dagger. "*Iä Tsathoggua,* Father of Night! *Iä G'noth-ykagga-ha!* Awaken with the bitter blood of this offering to crush our enemies!"

The Comanche dancers redoubled their savage ritual, hurtling over the fire or beating their heads into the ground until the bricks were slick with blood. Many lay dead or dying before the fire. And many more succumbed to the final throes of the Backward Path, expelling their bones and raising twisting tentacle-arms to their new god in a blasphemous mockery of spiritual rebirth.

The floor beneath the pyramid groaned a long slow song of tortured stone that added a desperate urgency to the dance. Spreading webs of cracks shot through rotted masonry. The ledge was breaking apart under their feet, yet no one but Stickney took any notice.

And when he looked beyond it, out there in the perfect void that seemed at first to offer the only respite from carnage and horror—now he sensed that the boundless darkness was no longer an emptiness at all, but a *presence* that filled the void as nightmares fill sleep. It was no avatar or idol, but an incarnation of darkness itself, for unless Stickney had finally lost his mind, he now saw the guttering bonfire lights reflected in a pair of colossal, half-lidded eyes that watched in the gulf, drowsily mocking their fighting and dying and hungering to be filled with all that lived in the light.

Hull lunged up after Malakai with both knives upraised, but suddenly he stopped, just out of reach of the waiting, passive priest. Perhaps he saw it, too.

Something was wrong, but Hull could not read it in Malakai's well-defended mind. The blue-eyed monster could not help gloating as he thrust out his pallid chest to accept the blade. "Yes, kill me, Inigo Hull. Deliver me to Him, as the ritual demands. To awaken the sleeping Father of Night, his favored priest must be slain by another priest of the blood. The father must die by the hand of the son. Surely you can do this much?"

Hull looked at the knives, and then at the Kotsotekas band, dying or worse on the crumbling pyramid. Then he looked for some time into the void. He said nothing, did not move.

"If you will not play your role, then they will all still belong to Him. And if you die by my hand or your own, remember that your blood and soul are recorded in the dreaming engines of Tsath. We can keep bringing you back and trying it until you get it right."

Hull stood frozen for a long moment, but finally he sheathed his knives on his belt. "I am sick to death of killing you. If your gods were apt to trade blood for miracles, they would have awakened long ago. This nation is red and ripe with the blood of millions, and still they sleep."

Hull stood fast before the silently fuming Malakai. Stickney fought the urge to step between them, for a web of silent conflict seemed to weave the air between them in flexing nets of invisible force.

"No," Hull finally said, breathless but resolute, "I will not kneel to Tsathoggua. And neither will my people."

Stickney felt, rather than heard, a roaring voice speaking the Comanche tongue, too fast and too loud for him to understand any of it. But he was not the audience for the bolt of thought that stormed the cavern.

His sight was obscured by a flurry of overwhelming images, each striking with the force of a seizure: of men a mile in height riding on horses of fire over oceans of buffalo; of decorated dancers and storytellers leading a laughing band of families in a song of earth and sky; of an old, old woman teaching a little girl to care for a silent, pale baby with deep green eyes; of a fierce warrior launching long arrows from the back of a galloping horse, three at a time, as if to shoot down the sun.

In the blink of an eye he reminded them that they were the people of the horse, the masters of the plains, and the gentle finders of lost children. They were the children of the ones who walked away from the decadent decay of K'n-yan, and chose a harder, simpler life. They were the Comanche, and they would not bow to a beast or the god of beasts.

Instantly the mad, raw-throated chanting behind him fell silent. The surviving dancers froze and then shrank to the bloody stone steps, weeping and gasping for breath.

Malakai fought for the strength to stab Hull's eyes out. Though he did not move, his narrow chest heaved and bucked, and his pale face darkened with scarlet blossoms of broken blood vessels spreading like spilled wine under his skin. "No, you are but a child . . . you could not possibly know how to walk in their minds . . ."

"But I have had a great teacher in you." Hull grated. Despite the strain in his pained expression, he pressed forward, driving Malakai back toward the high altar. "That first time we met, you walked through *my* mind, and every time since, you've searched me to find if I was mad enough yet to join you. But every time we met, I learned more of how you did it, and I learned more of what you are.

"Did you really think it would come as a surprise to me to learn I was of the blood of K'n-yan? Did you think it would break me and remake me into you? I was a tool to you, as you are a tool to the evil gods you serve. The Comanche tried to give me a home when no one else would. They told me I was one of them, but I lost my way. When you showed me what I am, you reminded me of what I could have been, and could be still. Thank you for that."

The pyramid was littered with dozens of dead and dying bodies, and the transformed ones had seemingly slipped away, but the hundred and thirty or so survivors had begun to recollect themselves. Lifting wailing children and shouldering the old ones and the wounded, they limped down the steps of the pyramid. However their long road to the surface was blocked by another mob of naked, battered bodies that came shuffling to the foot of the pyramid bearing an object that flashed with blinding azure light.

Stickney rushed to get ahead of the Comanche in leaving, but he hid behind Hull when he saw the silent procession of *y'm-bhi* shambling up the steps of the pyramid toward the high altar.

The scorched and half-cremated undead slaves bore an even more haggard specimen on their shoulders like a conquering hero: one who, for all its grievous bodily wounds, was yet somehow alive. *"God damn you . . . Hull,"* the blackened husk of a man cried, and Stickney realized it was Tobin Roherty.

He got his treasure at last, Stickney thought.

Cradled in his arms was an enormous, oddly faceted crystal that glowed with a sinister indigo radiance so pure and hypnotic that it seemed to warp the air around it into the fleeting phantoms of screaming faces.

The same awful azure light gushed out of Tobin Roherty's eyeholes. Hull supposed that, if he had stolen the gemstone from the machines with which the people of Tsath resurrected themselves, then perhaps he'd become the last refuge for all the undead Indians trapped inside it. A thousand lunatic ghosts howled with his throat as the *y'm-bhi* bore him closer to the altar. "You treacherous sidewinder, *I'll see you in Hell—*"

"There are many hells," replied Hull. "I doubt we'll find ourselves in the same one." He turned to Malakai and bowed. "If your god must have a sacrifice, let us see what he makes of this one."

With Roherty screaming curses all the way, the *y'm-bhi* marched off the edge and plummeted into the void. The cracks in the pyramid became groaning fault lines. The outer edge of the pyramid crumbled away into the gulf. Stickney listened intently, not expecting to hear them hit the bottom, but he heard them hit, or get caught by something, much sooner than he expected.

Malakai screamed a wordless battle cry and flung himself upon Hull. The half-breed danced back and drew his knives to drive them both into Malakai's breast . . . then just as quickly dropped them and threw his arms wide, as the high priest fell upon him.

Like a rattler's strike, the dagger lanced out for Hull's throat, but he dodged it and caught Malakai in a fierce embrace. Almost one could have thought that Hull had forgiven everything and expressed only his love for his grandfather, until the bones of the medicine man's spine began to pop like corn in a fire. Malakai went limp in Hull's arms and dropped his dagger.

"If you had only given me a home and a name," Hull said, "I might have been yours, and eager to help you burn down the world."

"When I am gone," Malakai croaked, "He will call to you, in his greedy dreaming. The last one left who can wake Him now . . . you will never know peace . . ."

"When have I *ever* known peace?" Hull's laugh was bitter, but deep and loud with relief. "When have I ever asked for peace? If he calls, I will tell him what I have told you. He can't afford me."

Malakai gurgled and spat blood by way of reply. He tried to drag himself to the edge, but Hull held him tighter and twisted his neck until he sighed and finally died. He dissolved in Hull's arms in a churning cloud of blue smoke that wafted about as if desperate to take solid form again; but the granular mist dissipated on the noisome breeze of N'kai, which Hull darkly suspected was no wind at all, but some kind of belch.

Stickney whooped with joy, so great was his relief, but then he looked around and saw only a glowering Inigo Hull and a horde of painted Comanche refugees gathered around him.

"I won't tell anyone," Stickney stammered, "what I saw—"

Hull picked up the dagger and some other odd effects from the strange blue puddle where Malakai had died, and turned the full force of his gaze on Stickney's shivering form. The wounded Indian agent felt steel-tipped fingers tapping on the paper walls of his mind. "And what will you tell them?"

He bethought himself for a long moment before choosing his answer. "I will tell them that the Kotsotekas got lost, but we found them and led them home."

Hull looked into him for a long time, and then simply said, "Good. And Major Cawthorne?"

"I'll tell them I hope they find him someday. And to start looking in Mexico." Stickney stumbled, and Hull caught him as they began to climb the spiraling steps out of N'kai.

"That thing in the pit . . . Sa—"

"Never say it," Hull hissed.

Stickney felt light-headed and rushed to get it out before he fainted. "If it ever awakens—"

"Not in your lifetime, white man," said Inigo Hull. "But if that day ever comes, I will be waiting."

Hull helped Stickney to his feet, and together the two men staggered upwards, leading the refugees up the long trail to daylight.

Acknowledgments

"Black Wind" (as by Cody Winchester Goodellow) was first published as a chapbook by Perilous Press, 2013.

"Broken Bell" was first published as a serial on Shoggoth.net, December 2022.

"Forked Tongue" was first published in *Edge of Sundown*, ed. Kevin Ross and Brian M. Sammons (Chaosium, 2015).

"The Greedy Grave" was first published in *Creature Features*, ed. Duane Pesice (Planet X Publications, 2018).

"Shadow Empire" was originally published as "Unseen Empire" in *Cthulhu Unbound 3*, ed. David Conyers and Brian M. Sammons (Permuted Press, 2013).

www.ingramcontent.com/pod-product-compliance
Lightning Source LLC
Chambersburg PA
CBHW070030260626
47159CB00005B/1999